SHADOWMANCY

Jason Franks

SHADOWMANCY
Copyright © 2023 Jason Franks. All rights reserved.

Published by Outland Entertainment LLC
3119 Gillham Road
Kansas City, MO 64109

Founder/Creative Director: Jeremy D. Mohler
Editor-in-Chief: Alana Joli Abbott

ISBN: 978-1-954255616
EBOOK ISBN: 978-1-954255623
Worldwide Rights
Created in the United States of America

Editor: Scott Colby
Cover Illustration: Shannon Potratz
Cover Design: Jeremy Mohler
Interior Layout: Mikael Brodu

Printed and bound in the United States of America.

Visit **outlandentertainment.com** to see more, or follow us on our Facebook Page **facebook.com/ outlandentertainment/**

For Yuriko

Act I.

— THE KEY IN THE WALL —

E ven before I went to the Academy, my name was the source of my problems.

People would ask it of me, and I would tell them.

"Quay."

They would ask me again, and I would repeat myself.

"Like, what you put in a lock?"

"Quay." I did not offer them an alternative definition.

"What's your surname, Quay?"

"That is my surname."

"Then what's your Christian name?"

"I am not a Christian."

Then they would ask if I was trying to be funny. I was not. Humor is not something to which I am inclined. My interrogators would nod slowly and consider their next question, which would invariably be: "Where you from, Quay?"

"New York," I would reply.

I would hold the same conversation, again and again, with everybody I knew. Teachers and classmates and neighbors and curious strangers.

It was a game to them. I would hear them talking about me—on the sidewalks, on the stoops, in the lunchroom, and across the schoolyard. Sometimes they muttered, sometimes they snickered openly.

"What's your name? Where you from?"

"Quay. New York."

They were the only answers I had. Even if I had cared to find out more, I don't believe my parents would have told me.

My mother was a good mother, I suppose. Certainly, she did all of the motherly things required for such a designation. She clothed me and kept me clean and made sure that I was fed and sheltered. She kept me, period. She said all the things that mothers say to their children. It was only the volume of secrets she kept that was in disproportion. Not that she had any choice in the matter.

My mother never allowed me to wander more than two blocks from home. The house, the school, the market, the deli—that was the extent of my world. Every time I tried to sneak away, she would somehow intercept me. Some would say that my mother was always there for me, but in my specific circumstances it was literally uncanny.

Reading was my only escape. I hated school. I had no interest in playing with my schoolmates. I didn't want friends. I despised the television. But books...

Our house was crammed with books, and I read every one of them from cover to cover. I devoured the contents of the school library like a swarm of locusts. Fiction, non-fiction. Magazines, journals, newspapers, comics. Manuals, textbooks, scholarly tracts, sale catalogues. Reading was my only escape, and I resented anything that came between me and that activity. My intellect was the only part of me allowed to wander.

By the time I was ten, I'd given up all hope of freedom. My entire universe was contained inside that two-block radius.

Unless my father was home.

—— ⊂ ● ⊃ ——

My father traveled for his work. He was a teacher, a professor at some remote, but prestigious, university. That was all anybody knew about him, and nobody cared to know more. At the time I did not think that was strange.

I can't say that I liked my father, but I did look forward to his visits. During the few short weeks of the year he was home, things were different in the house. My mother was different.

It was as though someone had flipped a switch on her, as though she had been turned off. She would sit in front of the TV, or lie in bed and sleep, almost from the moment that he came home. My mother would greet my father when he came and went, but

I never saw them hold a conversation. Only when he left did she return to her usual self. She still looked young, but she was frayed on the inside. Worn through by doing her duty to the exclusion of all else. She had no more friends than I did.

I had read enough books and glimpsed enough TV to think that I understood the adult world. I thought she was drinking or popping pills, and I knew it was my father's fault—although I never saw my father do anything bad to her. He never so much as raised his voice.

What he had done to her was far worse than I could have guessed.

Some people are fearsome because they are fierce. They are commanding and assertive; they demand that you acknowledge their presence and their mastery. Others are fearsome because they are quiet. They demand nothing from you, but you know their mastery yet. My father was a quiet man.

Our house was always a quiet place. There was seldom conversation between my mother and me, and my father spoke even less. The only thing he required of us was that we kept the record player on. Always Mozart. To my knowledge those records were the only pleasure he permitted himself, though he could have taken whatever he wanted.

I never learned to appreciate music, but those records moved me in a way that I have seldom felt. Perhaps it was just that I associated Mozart so strongly with my father's presence. Perhaps at those times I was happy. Perhaps it was just the thrill of fear. Even now I cannot rightly identify the emotion. Although his visits were supposed to be vacations, my father would spend most of his time in his study, working. My mother would rouse herself to cook and clean and do whatever was necessary to look after the house. Neither one of them had attention for me, but I did not need or want it. I had more time to read when my father was at home.

Some nights, when he became restless, my father would leave the house. He would be gone for hours. Sometimes, he would take me with him.

Together we would walk the streets. Ride the subways. There was never a destination, just a circuit that ended where it had begun. I lived for the journey, but I dreaded the return home. We traveled in silence. I knew better than to ask questions of him.

Teacher or not, my father was a man of few words. He would speak only to issue instructions: "Give me two tokens," to the lady in the subway booth, or "Come along now," if I lingered too long at the window of a bookstore. Nothing more.

We stayed on the streets. Walking, just walking. Always walking. We never browsed inside any stores or stopped in any restaurants or cafés.

I came to believe that there was some meaning to these journeys that I could not understand. Some pattern described by the route we took, by names of the places we went and the trains we rode; some hidden significance in even my father's few utterances. I did not want affection from him. All I wanted was meaning.

After a couple of weeks in Brooklyn, my father would pack his duffle bag and go. He never said goodbye to me or to my mother. He'd be gone for six months or more. He never told us when to expect him back, and we never did expect him. It usually took a full day for my mother to recover herself. I never tried to sneak outside my assigned territory during this time. I suppose I was recovering too. We didn't discuss it. We didn't discuss my father or anticipate his comings and goings. It was beyond our control and beyond our ken.

When I turned thirteen, I decided that the next time he came and went, I would go with him.

I didn't ask permission. My father was not a man you could ask for things. Furthermore, I knew that if he explicitly refused me, I would never be able to leave. I would be confined inside that two-block radius forever.

From the living room window of our apartment, I watched him walk down the steps. The Mozart record was still playing. My father had his duffle slung over his shoulder, and he did not look back. I was sure he knew that I was watching him, so I waited until he had turned the corner before I went out the door after him.

It was a summer night. All I had on were jeans and a t-shirt and sneakers. I thought myself fully prepared for whatever journey was to come. I had the sum total of my earthly wealth in my hip pocket—a five-dollar bill I had liberated from my mother's purse and one dollar eighty in coins that I had collected from the change slot in the vending machine in the school cafeteria, from the gutter, from inside the sofa.

Six dollars and eighty cents. I did not think it would last me long, but I hoped that it would demonstrate my self-sufficiency if my father called it into question.

I shadowed my father, moving past the darkened shop fronts, the alley mouths, the tenement stoops. We passed the deli, then the school. This was the furthest I had ever been, unaccompanied.

There was nobody about.

I watched him go down into the subway station. I did not turn the corner in time to see him put a token into the turnstile, but I was certain he had not stopped to buy one on his way down. Perhaps he already had the token with him. I thought it more likely that the turnstile had simply let him through.

As soon as I judged it safe, I slipped under the turnstile. I did not want to risk losing him while I bought a token, and I did not want him to hear the turnstile twist.

I followed him up to the platform. Here there were people. A street girl. A drunken merchant banker. A bum who was likely responsible for the reek at the bottom of every ramp. Perhaps he was marking his territory, like a dog. Perhaps he just used whichever wall was closest when he had the urge to piss. I was homeless now, too, I supposed. I felt the urge to urinate.

I boarded the train in the carriage behind the one my father chose. I didn't know where it was going.

I didn't care. I just wanted to go somewhere. Away from the house, away from the deli, away from the school, away from what was left of my mother. It wasn't that I wanted to be with my father, it was just that he was the only person I knew who ever went anywhere.

———<●>———

My father disembarked at a downtown station. I followed him out of the train and up the stairs to the street.

The city was full of people, despite the late hour, and it took me a moment to locate him in the sudden crowd. My father had already crossed the road and was striding on, past a row of brightly lit storefronts. These were nothing like the shabby grocery marts and pawn shops and pizza parlors of my Brooklyn neighborhood. These shops showed jewelry, watches, suits, and cocktail dresses behind armored glass windows. There were brand names on the awnings and limousines in the streets. My father had never brought me to this part of town in our late-night wanderings.

He seemed a different man walking these streets, dressed in his dark suit, his black hair tied back into a ponytail and the old duffle bag slung over his shoulder. For all that I resembled him, he seemed a stranger to me then. He looked sinister, capable of both wonders and horrors. More capable than I could ever hope to be.

Around a corner we came to a street lined with fancy restaurants. Men in tuxedos, women in evening gowns. They might as well have been space aliens. People did not dress like this in my neighborhood. My father, in contrast, looked as if he belonged here–a prince who had come to survey a distant part of his kingdom. He might have owned every place, every person, every car and tree and streetlamp within his vision.

My father turned abruptly and disappeared into an alley I hadn't even noticed was there. I followed him.

At the end of the alley was a decaying old building. A sign in the window named it the "Key in the Wall Ristorante Italiano." The light behind the glass door was warmer and duller than the cold, bright lights on the main street. I pulled the door open and went inside.

Plastic tables, covered with cheap checkered table-cloths. Laminated menus, paper napkins. Jars of Parmesan cheese and chili flakes. Guttering candles in mismatched glass holders. There was no maître d' to intercept me at the door.

None of the few patrons looked up at my father as he passed by them. He turned into a corridor. A sign indicated that it led to the gentlemen's room.

The corridor was unpainted. Exposed pipes ran the length of both unplastered walls. Cockroaches skittered in every darkened recess. My father picked his way between the stacks of spare chairs, potted plants, broken appliances, boxes of non-perishable kitchen supplies. He moved past the restrooms and went on to the end of the hallway, which was strung with beads like the entrance to a head shop or a pornographic bookstore. I followed him through.

As I passed through the bead curtain, my surroundings became...strange. The exposed pipes bent and branched and pulsed as I went on. The walls crumbled into loose bricks and cement dust, and the linoleum floor buckled beneath me, leading down into a darkness that was neither a cavern nor a pit, neither void nor abyss. It was deeper than the ocean, but shallower than the sky. It was a space that lay between other spaces.

In later years I would come to know it well.

As I followed the path, my field of vision narrowed. I could see no further ahead than my father. I prayed he would not look behind him. But a part of me wished that he would, and take my hand.

My father slung the duffle bag off his shoulder and carried it in one hand. That was when his clothing began to change. The weave of his suit jacket rippled, and the pinstripes ran out. The collar rolled down into a tabard; the shoulders softened, and the cuffs drooped into scallops. He went on without breaking stride, now clad in a sweeping robe.

The duffle bag grew legs and became a beast: a quadruped with the armor of a lizard and the grace of a cat. It loped ahead at the end of a length of chain that had once been the duffle's handle.

A surge of exultation drove the fear and loneliness from me. Perhaps I would die here. Perhaps I would live to find some new world, some new life. In either case, I had won my fondest desire. I had escaped my two-block prison.

Beneath my feet the linoleum became concrete, then bare earth, then loose rock. The path began to rise again, bending one way and then the other. The stone became smooth, and then polished.

Slowly the way spread open again, and the space around me unfolded into a bright, open sky. With my field of vision restored, I found that I had emerged from the interstices to a plateau high in the mountains. I did not know which mountains they might be, that were walking distance from Manhattan. It was cold enough that I immediately began to shiver. There was no snow on the rocky ground, although all of the neighboring peaks were white with it.

A sea of clouds, golden in the twilight, prevented me from seeing the valley floor below. When I looked behind me, I could see no indication of the strange path that had brought me there.

Cut marble steps rose from the far side of the plateau, leading up to a ziggurat carved directly into the mountainside. It resembled a Cambodian temple or a Tibetan monastery, but there was something Brutalist about its lines, which were sheer and sharp and severe. Even in the dusk, light reflected harshly from the bare white stone, making it hard to look upon the building directly. I wondered how brightly it shone at night.

————⟨●⟩————

As my father mounted the steps with the lizard-cat restrained on a tight leash, a figure resolved at the top of the stairs. It was a tall, elderly man, clad in robes that were cut more simply than my father's.

"Ah, Professor Quay."

My father stopped dead in his tracks, but when he replied it was in his usual, uninflected tone. "Chancellor."

The Chancellor's hair was long and white and his face seamed and gaunt, but he stood as straight as a soldier on parade. Only the rectangular glasses resting on his nose gave any hint of infirmity.

I had never seen such a visage before. To this day, I have never seen that cast of features duplicated, or that set of expressions. The Chancellor was from some race long gone from the world to which I belong. Some race that was no longer represented anywhere–not even in Brooklyn.

"Let us not waste time on pleasantries, Professor Quay," said the Chancellor. "I know what you have done."

"And what crime is so heinous that you have seen fit to name me for it?"

"You have kept a family, Professor. Worse, you have attempted to conceal them from us."

It was the only time in my life I had ever seen my father hesitate. "It has taken you thirteen years to penetrate my wards."

The Chancellor shook his head. "Professor Quay, *I* did not penetrate your wards. *He* did."

My father turned and looked down the steps. The expression that came upon his face when he saw me there was not a kind one. But he said nothing. Instead, he turned back to the Chancellor and cocked his head. "So what?"

The lizard-cat at his side hissed. Something dripped through its teeth and sizzled on the marble stairs. Nitric acid.

"So what?" he said again. "I remain the greatest magician this Academy has yet produced. When you are gone, I will be the Chancellor. All the faculty know it."

The Chancellor stared at my father. "I am not going anywhere, Professor."

A breeze stirred the Chancellor's robes. My father fell.

He landed, sprawling, on his back. His head struck the edge of a step, and I heard bone crack. My father lay where he had fallen, dressed once more in his suit, with the duffle bag crumpled beside him. His eyes were rolled back in his head, and blood dribbled from his mouth.

But it was not the fall that had taken him. His face had been empty before he had hit the ground.

The Chancellor turned to me. "Now then," he said. "Come here, boy. I wish to examine you."

I mounted the stairs as my father had before me. I stopped with my feet at the same level as his head. I became aware of more figures arrayed behind the Chancellor, but his eyes transfixed me and I could not so much as glance at them. I have never seen eyes like those, before or since. The irises were dark behind the lenses of his glasses, but they cast some kind of colorless radiance that chased the shadows from his features.

"You are a bold one, young master Quay. Talented, as your father before you. Would you study here at the Academy? Would you seek the Mysteries?"

"Yes."

"It will not be easy for you. Perhaps you will find power here, perhaps only misery. If you choose to study at the Academy you will have to give up your freedom. Your place in the world. If you fail, you may never earn them back."

This did not seem like much of a sacrifice. I had never been free. I had never had a place in the world. "All right."

"You will also have to relinquish your name."

"All right."

The Chancellor peered down at me over the rims of his spectacles. "Convince me, Master Quay. Why should I believe that you are willing to give up the name that your father, apparently, could not?"

"Because I don't want it."

"And why is that?"

I did not look down at my father. I knew he could neither see nor hear me. "It belongs to him."

"I see." The Chancellor drew himself up again. "Your father..." He inhaled deeply as he considered his words. "Your father did not keep you because he loved you. Do you understand me, boy? Your father kept you because you were his property."

"I understand."

The Chancellor straightened his glasses. "The Academy does not permit families," he said. "The skills we teach here are far too dangerous. We cannot risk our Arts falling subject to some *dynasty*." He looked at my father. "Even base heredity is a corrupting influence. It is crucial that the discipline remains pure. Do you understand me?"

"Yes."

The Chancellor continued to regard me. "You should not be here. You should not exist. I am breaking the rules by allowing you this, but I will not make you pay for your father's failings."

At the time, it seemed like he was being generous.

I would give him cause to regret it.

Act 2.

— BLOODLINES —

The Chancellor showed me to an empty cell. The door was made of wood and had no lock. Angled-down windows were set almost at ceiling height.

"This is your room."

There was absolutely nothing in the room. No closet, no desk, no bed. Not a speck of dust or a smudge of grime. Nothing.

"My room?"

"Yours," said the Chancellor. "You can use it for whatever purposes you wish."

"What...purposes?"

"Sleeping, of course. Private study. Storage. Anything else you'd care to."

I looked around the empty room again. I tried to think of something to say that wouldn't be stating the obvious. "It's not very well-equipped."

"You can fill it with anything you wish."

"Where can I get...things?"

The Chancellor shrugged. "Anywhere you can find them."

"How can I get...anywhere?"

"Any Way that you can."

"I thought I was to be confined to the grounds of the Academy."

"No," said the Chancellor. "If you can find safe passage you are free to come and go as you please." His tone made me doubt this was as easily accomplished as said.

The Chancellor turned to leave.

I thought about calling him back. I wanted to ask what I was supposed to do next, where I was supposed to go. But I did not. He had made it clear that he would not answer my questions in a way that would impart useful information.

I waited for two minutes before I peeked outside of my room. Night seemed to fall the moment that I opened the door. The darkness was impenetrable, and I had no way of making a light.

I returned to my room and went to sleep on the cold marble floor.

When I awoke the next morning, I sat in my empty room and waited, but nobody came to deliver instructions about what I should do next.

I decided that I would explore the place. It was certainly better than sitting there staring at the four blank walls. I was hungry and thirsty and dirty, and already I was bored.

I spent perhaps an hour wandering through the white stone corridors. The ceilings were high, and the floors were spotlessly clean. There was little to distinguish one hallway from the next. Only the doors showed any variation. Some were plain wood, like mine, but others were made of steel, glass, or stone. Some were inlaid with precious metals; others were constructed from the shells of sea creatures, or the hides of animals.

Most doors had locks on them: deadbolts, padlocks, combination dials, or valves that needed to be cranked with a lever. Some of them had keypads or thumbprint scanners, although I saw no indications that the Academy was wired for electricity. Some of the doorways were sealed with the same white stone as the walls.

The only doors I could open were the bare wooden ones. Inevitably, they lead to empty rooms. Aside from the orientation of the windows, there was nothing to distinguish them from my own.

Eventually I came to the shower room.

It was a wide chamber with a slightly convex floor. Runnels had been cut along the perimeter, leading down to small open drains in each of the corners. There were no showerheads, or even taps; water just poured from holes in the wall. I wondered at the source of the water. Were there pipes beneath the floor? Was there a cistern somewhere deep beneath us? I did not think so. There was just a room where water ran endlessly out of the walls.

I scrubbed myself in the hot water as best I could. I did not have soap or a towel. Clammy inside my sweat-stained clothes, I set off to see what else I could find.

After more wandering, I thought I could hear a buzzing. At first I wasn't sure if it was just the sound of blood in my ears, but as I proceeded down the corridor it began to resemble human voices. Once I turned the corner, I discovered the source of the noise.

An open archway led into a wide, colonnaded room, carved from the same white stone as the rest of the Academy. Huge windows flooded the room with the bright light of the morning. The sky outside was a washed-out blue, and the clouds were a golden haze.

It did not have the appearance of a classroom or a lecture theater, but a professor in robes stood at one end of it, holding forth to a motley group of a dozen students.

There was no furniture in the room, not even a chalkboard or a lectern. There were no desks. The students had no books or writing implements; they just lounged about, listening to the professor, or not, as they felt like it. Most of them did not.

The professor was a middle-aged man dressed in robes of a plainer design than those the Chancellor wore. He sported a stubbly beard and big, tear-drop-shaped glasses. He did not pause his lecture to acknowledge my late arrival.

"...is a reductive process. You must separate the object from the identity that defines it in the universe before you can operate upon it. Once you have removed the object's name, you may then begin to pare down the concepts that give it form and purpose until it is malleable to your will. Only then can you begin to change its nature."

A dark-skinned boy about my age sat cross-legged before the professor, nodding his head. He had dark, ruddy skin and his scalp had been shaved bald. Egyptian, I surmised, though he looked more like a fresco from an ancient tomb than any Egyptian I had ever met in person. He wore a rumpled suit and an open-collared shirt. His feet were bare.

The Egyptian looked over his shoulder at me when I entered the room, then returned his attention to the professor. He raised his hand.

"Yes, Acolyte?"

"Is that why we are unnamed, Professor? When we are accepted to the Academy?" I could tell that the Egyptian already knew the answer. I had the quick impression that this teacher had been newly appointed, and the Egyptian was trying to curry favor.

"Yes. Your parents named you before you were a person. Their purpose in so doing was to join you to their family line and to pin certain qualities upon you. To associate you with the qualities that have been demonstrated by others who are, or were, so named.

"A name pins you to the consensual reality of humankind. A name prevents you from transcending that reality, from seeing the Mysteries that lie beyond that reality's horizons. If your Self is not free, it can never solve the Mystery. If your Self is named, it can never ascend to power."

I raised my hand and approached the group.

"Ah, the new boy." I did not like his tone, but at least somebody had acknowledged my presence. "Sit."

I sat on the floor and crossed my legs.

"Now, you may ask your question."

"Professor, will you teach us to use this...power?" It did not seem like a foolish question.

A girl with a spider tattoo on her neck giggled. Her hair was dark and long and curly. Her eyes were just as dark. I thought she might be Greek.

The professor stared at me. "I am teaching it to you now."

"Yes, but, when will we learn how to use it? To cast spells, and such?"

The professor shook his head and then looked down to the Egyptian. "Acolyte," he said, "explain to the new boy why the Academy does not teach the 'casting' of 'spells.'"

A boy sitting behind me snickered. When I turned around to see who laughed, he smirked and slowly raised his middle finger. American, like me. He had light, frizzy hair, buzzed on the sides. He was smaller than me, and at least a year younger.

The Egyptian looked over his shoulder at me again and grinned. "Power cannot be taught. It must be earned. Power cannot be given. It may only be taken."

"Thank you, Acolyte." The professor turned to me. "Are you satisfied with that answer, new boy?"

I shook my head.

"Well, that in itself is a lesson." The professor looked around the class. I found myself thinking of him as Professor Thieu, although I had not consciously sought to assign him a name. "I believe that we are done for today. New boy, if you desire a midday meal, I suggest you follow your classmates to the Refectory."

It was the first and last time Thieu told me anything overtly useful.

———⟨●⟩———

The Refectory was a room full of trestle tables and plastic chairs. The cheap furnishings made the colonnaded walls look fake, like a matte background for a cheap movie.

Food was set out on a bench at the end of the room near the windows. I could not tell who had set out the meal for us; there were no servitors or cooks in evidence.

I lined up with the others and, when it was my turn, I spooned some steaming broth from a tureen into a bowl. It was thick with noodles, vegetables, and some pale meat. There was no discernible aroma.

A cabinet nearby offered knives, forks, chopsticks, spoons, tongs, and a variety of implements I did not recognize. I took a spoon. Then, on consideration, I took a knife as well. It was blunt.

I found a seat at an empty trestle on the far side of the room from my classmates. I had no desire to befriend any of the other students. I had never been permitted friends before, and I didn't feel the need to change that now.

When the Egyptian set down his tray across the table from me, I thought it a sign of aggression. I adjusted my grip on the knife and looked him in the eye.

The Egyptian looked at the knife and smiled. "If you were intending to use that as a weapon, I suspect you'd have better luck with the spoon," he said.

I put down the butter knife, and he settled into his chair.

"Your father used to teach us, you know," said the Egyptian. His name came to me unbidden: Saad.

"Well, that's more than he did for me." I looked enough like my father that I did not have to wonder how Saad knew who I was.

"He brought you here, didn't he?" Saad started to slurp the noodles from his bowl, holding it near his face and shoveling with his chopsticks.

"He didn't bring me. I followed him."

Saad set his bowl back on the table and replied around a mouthful of food. "It was forbidden for him to keep a family."

"And he was punished for it."

We ate in silence. I spooned pieces of meat and vegetable out of the broth. The noodles were too difficult to manage.

"Did you really follow him? How did he come here?"

"He walked. There was a...path."

Saad nodded. "A Way," he said, twirling some noodles around his chopsticks. "Did you pass through a Door first?"

"Many doors," I replied, although I didn't fully understand the question. "How did *you* get here?"

Saad shrugged. "I was chosen, like all the other acolytes here. The Chancellor came to me in a dream and offered me a place. I accepted. When I awoke, I was here."

"You alone?"

"Just me and the Chancellor. No two students arrive on the same day."

I looked across at the American boy with the buzz-cut who had flipped me off in class. He was sitting at a table with three others who seemed to find everything he said hugely amusing. When he saw me looking, he pointed his left index finger at me like a gun and pretended to shoot me. Boudreaux.

I turned back to Saad, who was also looking at the gunman. "What about *him*?"

"Him?" Saad shrugged ruefully. "Stay away from him. He's been here longer than anyone else in our cohort, and he's still the youngest."

"What does that mean?" I asked.

"It means he's particularly gifted. His talent ripened early, and he was harvested sooner than the rest of us."

"Precocious is not the same as talented."

"Oh, he's talented," said Saad. "There's no doubt about that. Talented and insecure. A dangerous combination."

I doubted these qualities were as rare at the Academy as Saad made them sound. "If you say so."

Saad quirked a smile and regarded me through hooded eyes. "Don't cross him. He'll fuck you up."

I returned Saad's gaze evenly. "I'm the newest arrival in the school. I have no knowledge or power. I am no threat to him."

"Ah." Saad tilted his head. "It's not the recency of your arrival that threatens him, it's the manner of it."

"Oh?"

"You are the only student who has found a place here without being chosen."

"It was not intentional."

"Nevertheless. You came by yourself, and the Chancellor still took you in. That means you have talent. Moreover, you have something nobody else here does."

I scowled.

Saad tapped his neck with his free hand. "You have a bloodline."

"Everybody has a bloodline," I said. "The only difference is that everybody here knows mine."

Saad made a motion from his jugular vein that indicated spurting fluid. "Blood will out, whether you like it or not," he said. "The only question is just how profusely you will bleed."

After lunch Saad showed me to another class, which was held in a different part of the building to the earlier lecture. This classroom was smaller and darker, with fewer windows and without the pillars and arches. There were fewer students here, too.

Unlike Thieu, who stood and lectured to a roomful of indolent students, this teacher knelt in the middle of the room and the acolytes sat in an orderly semicircle in front of her. Although she never told us where to sit, we all found our places well enough: Boudreaux on the far left of the teacher, with Saad beside him, and me on the far right. The girl with the spider tattoo sat near the middle. Arakne.

It was difficult to judge the teacher's age: her skin was fair and unlined, but her hair was more gray than black. Her robe was belted with a wide and elaborate sash that made it resemble a kimono.

"Acolytes, you have come here, to the Academy, because you want the power to change the world," she said. "Because you think that nature is an impediment to your will. You believe reality opposes your desires. But this is not the case."

She spoke with a staccato Japanese inflection. The other students addressed her not as Professor, but as Sensei. I named her Maruyama.

"You live in reality. You are real. Flesh and blood. You are a natural human, and you cannot exist outside of a reality that is compatible with that into which you were born."

Some of the students were nodding, including Saad. Boudreaux sat with his arms folded.

"You have come here seeking supernatural powers, but you must understand that there can be no supernature without some baseline natural order." She let her gaze pan across the semicircle, left to right. "This nature goes beyond the world of matter. Reality has a psychological dimension. The mind and its constructions–its ideas–are objectively real things, for all that they are immaterial."

"If an idea is a real thing, then show me one," scoffed Boudreaux.

"An idea is a quantum of information which can be communicated from one mind to another. An idea can initiate, and replicate, and translate, and mutate. An idea can influence the material world. Of course, ideas are real."

Arakne spoke up. "Ideas give rise to Art."

Maruyama showed neither approval nor disapproval at the interruption. "Art is the process of making material those ideas or desires. Art is where nature and magic intersect."

I was not certain I believed the lesson. I thought art was a pointless distraction, and I did not want to study it. I did not want to study nature. I wanted to learn magic. I did not then understand that art and magic are one and the same.

"The power you seek here, at the Academy, will enable you to manipulate nature," said Maruyama. "The better you understand the natural world, the better your art will be. The more precisely you direct your will...the more direct the Art you conjure with...the less energy you will need to achieve your work. The best art is not an exercise in power, but in design."

Boudreaux shook his head scornfully and muttered, "Power will overcome knowledge and design every time."

Maruyama stared at a point above Boudreaux's right shoulder. He shifted uncomfortably and looked away. "Power is finite," she said. "There is a limit to the amount of power an individual can channel. But *knowledge*? One can learn to the end of one's days, and every fact, every datum, every connection will increase one's ability to work one's Art."

The lesson ended there, and I was glad of it, but I knew that I would attend Maruyama's class again.

————⟨●⟩————

The food in the Refectory was always the same. Breakfast, lunch, and dinner—noodles in a flavorless broth, with vegetables and chewy protein that might have been meat and might have been soy.

I was just beginning my meal when Saad joined me at my table. I scowled at him but offered no protest. He was still my best source of information.

"How was your first day at the Academy?" he asked brightly.

I chewed my mouthful slowly and then swallowed. "I don't know," I replied. "I still don't understand anything."

Saad laughed. "You come to this Academy to learn the Mysteries," he said, imitating Professor Thieu's sonorous voice. "You must solve them for yourself, if you are to solve them at all."

"Makes you wonder why they conduct classes."

Saad drew a clump of noodles from his bowl and held them hanging from his chopsticks. "In class, we are taught the theories and philosophies of the Academy, but if you want to learn its secrets..." The noodles began to writhe like tendrils. He grinned.

"If you want to learn its secrets, you will have to steal them."

I'm sure the shock in my voice was audible. "From where?"

"From the professors, of course. And the students. They can be convinced to part with their knowledge, if you make it worth their while." Saad stuffed the noodles into his mouth and chewed contentedly.

"What kind of prices are we talking?"

Saad shrugged. "Depends on who's asking. Blood, allegiance, friendship, money, other favors..."

"Why bring us here if they will not teach us?"

"Oh, they are teaching us, all right. They are teaching us to think, to scheme, to keep secrets, and to strategize."

"They are controlling the knowledge. They are keeping it from us," I replied.

"They are controlling us, my friend. How else can you regulate a group of adepts with so much power at their disposal? Politics. Tangle them in an economy of obligations. Force them to regulate themselves."

I looked around the Refectory. It was empty now, but for one or two robed faculty members and a handful of students. I did not recognize any of them from either of my classes. They looked older than me and Saad.

"What happens to those who don't make the grade?"

"There's no 'making it,'" Saad replied. "There's no 'graduation.' We are students here for as long as we can bear it. The best of us will be elevated to faculty.

Some will give up and leave. Others will remain students until they die."

"So there *is* a way out of here?"

"If you want to leave you might bargain with someone in the faculty for safe passage home. But think twice before you ask, because you will never be able to find your way back here."

"Where is this place, anyway?"

Saad shrugged. "Atlantis? Tibet? The moon? Nobody knows the answer to that question."

"Then how can anyone come or go from this place?" What I really wanted to know was if the Way by which my father had led me here was accessible to others, or was at least known to them.

Saad was too subtle a player to give me the answer I sought. "There are plenty of other ways, if you have the Art," he said. "Or if you have friends who do."

I wondered if Saad had any such friends. I did not think so. Perhaps that was why he had sought me out. "What happens to those who quit?"

"As I understand it, most of them give up the Art and take their names back," replied Saad.

"And those who do not?"

"I don't know." Saad shrugged. "They do whatever they want, I guess. The only stricture upon them is that they may not teach the Naming Art. The Academy holds that exclusive right."

"Is this a school or a marketplace?"

Saad grinned. "It is both, my friend," he said. "If you want to learn the Naming Art you must beg, borrow, and steal for it, like all the rest of us." He wiped his chin with his fingers. "I am willing to trade you, if you like. A small working, just to get you started."

"I've got six dollars eighty and the clothes on my back."

"Ha," he replied. "And here I thought you were going to offer me your friendship."

I stared at him. "Does that have worth, here?"

"Not really."

I had finished my noodles, and I began to spoon up what was left of the broth. It was still very bland. I didn't want to ask Saad if there were condiments; I already knew what his answer would be. If I couldn't conjure them myself, I would have to bargain for them.

Saad sucked down the last of his meal and looked up at me brightly. "So? Are you interested?"

"In what?"

"In trade. I will teach you, say..." Saad did something with his face that flexed his nostrils as he inhaled. "Laundry. I will teach you a laundry spell."

"For six dollars eighty?"

"Six dollars eighty is a high price," he replied, "if it is all you possess."

I agreed to Saad's bargain. At least my first spell would be something useful.

———⟨●⟩———

The laundry spell was easy. Name the garment, name the dirt. Name the dirt separate from the garment and you are left with clean clothing and an oily cloud of skin flakes, crumbs, dust, and other residue.

A small working like that did not require a lot of energy: a degree of concentration, a squeeze of willpower. A handful of joules. The capacitance of the human body was more than sufficient to effect the change.

"The names are the most important part. Grammar doesn't matter," Saad told me. "Use whatever syntax you find most expedient. Whatever verbs. The important thing is that you clearly articulate what you want to happen to the named objects."

As I watched Saad execute the spell, I found that I could sense his workings if I paid close attention. With time and practice these senses would become more acute.

The laundry spell wasn't gentle on the garments. Saad taught me an additional cantrip to repair small damage. Name the garment, remove the name, then reinforce the weave of the fibers and re-apply the name. It left the clothing rumpled and stale, but clean.

The laundry spell had cost me all of my worldly wealth, and what value did it hold? Back in Brooklyn I could have walked into a laundromat and achieved the same thing for a handful of quarters.

Perhaps I should have bargained for a bar of soap.

I quickly became frustrated with Professor Thieu's classes. Sensei Maruyama spoke freely on diverse topics, with continuity and with a desire to see that her audience understood what she was teaching, but Thieu was deliberately obscure. He would cite historical examples and explain their significance from different philosophical outlooks, but the message was always the same. No wonder the other students–except for Saad–had given up paying attention.

I waited until Thieu's monologue was winding down before I raised my hand.

"Yes, Acolyte?" I supposed this was a promotion from "New Boy."

"Professor, you speak of the necessity to name the objects before you can exercise power over them, but you have not spoken of the source of this power. What kind of energies do we employ in our workings?"

"Ah," said Thieu. He seemed more than a little surprised at my question. "I see that you have been attending my counterpart's classes."

"I have."

"Well, do not let her confuse you. She teaches you about base reality. I am teaching you to look beyond."

"But there is an energy transfer, is there not?"

Thieu scowled at me. "Energy is required for any kind of transformation," he said.

"Does Art require a special kind of energy?"

Thieu snorted. "Energy is energy," he said. "Whether it comes from the sun, or the wind, or electrical charge, or the splitting of an atom. There is energy to be harnessed in every breath of air, every speck of dust, every glance of sunlight."

"Potential energy," I said.

Thieu nodded grudgingly. "A practitioner from the Academy is one who can channel that potential through himself and direct it through a logical framework. We transform the natural order by imposing this framework upon it, by naming or unnaming the parts that we wish to alter in sequence."

"Like an electrical circuit, in which you need to direct current through its component parts?"

"The Naming Art is more than mere circuitry," sniffed Thieu, but he did not elaborate. For my part, I could see no reason that a circuit design should not be considered a work of art.

"Are there other disciplines?" I asked. I had plenty more questions to ask while the professor was in a mood to answer. "How are their practices different to ours?"

Thieu made a dismissive noise in his sinus cavity. "Other disciplines are less precise. Less stable. Their practitioners must use metaphors or stories instead of proper names. Symbols and associations. Fiction and lies. Few of them know where true Art ends and where superstition begins."

"They keep their names."

"Correct. We are unnamed, and so we may observe the world from outside of its context. Other practitioners are limited by parallax and perspective, and this, in turn, limits the energies available to them. They must scrounge power from obvious sources. Ley lines, car batteries, solar panels. Or they may bargain for it from people or entities that are able to channel it for them.

"This is the reason the Academy stands above the other schools and colleges–the hedge witches and street magicians and gutter adepts. The Naming Art gives us the ability to work power without indirecting it through fantasy and delusion."

I nodded slowly. I did not know what 'indirecting' meant. I did not know if it was true, but Thieu certainly believed that our discipline was superior to all others.

"Have you any more questions, Acolyte, or is your curiosity sated for the time being?"

"Thank you, Professor." I knew that he had answered as much as he was willing to. I did not feel especially grateful.

Act 3.

— THE BOOK OF NAMES —

I spent most of my free time during those first weeks exploring the grounds of the Academy.

Despite the altitude, the weather was always fine and warm. The skies remained clear, and the wind never rose beyond a gentle breeze. I could see snow on the slopes below the plateau upon which the Academy sat, but there was none on the peak above.

The air became distinctly colder the further I went from the main building as the working that maintained the climate diminished in strength. The end to the Way my father had used to come and go from the Academy was chillier than I remembered.

There was nothing obvious to indicate the location of the Door, but I knew it when I found it. There was a feeling of pressure in my calves, in my fingers, behind my eyes. It felt like a place where I could slip through a gap in the world and disappear into darkness.

The buildings of the Academy had a tiered architecture, but there were no stairs inside it. Some corridors led up or down to different levels without obvious changes in gradient. It was difficult to know how high you were inside the structure if you were not in a room with a view to the outside. There were no interior windows, but a system of skylights and the arrangement of the corridors kept the building lit during the daylight hours.

The halls were very quiet. Perhaps in times past it had been thronged with adepts, but in my time there they were mostly empty. Or perhaps it was always that way: a place of study too big to be filled. I had no idea how many students were housed there. Beyond my own peers and our two teachers I rarely observed robed faculty members moving about the premises. I had not seen the Chancellor since my first day.

Exploring the place, I found mostly corridors and locked doors, with few actual destinations. If there was a kitchen where the food served in the Refectory was prepared, I never located it. I found no study hall, no rooms furnished with desks and chairs, no place that offered paper or writing implements. Most disappointing of all, I did not find a library.

There were terraces on three sides of the building. Those on the eastern and western faces were empty save for a handful of uncomfortable stone benches, but the northern terrace was the site of the aeroponic garden; a maze of trellises that hung suspended above the marble flooring. It was the only green place in the Academy.

Vegetation twisted through the wooden frames; roots tangled in the mesh with foliage blooming above it. Water and nutrients were administered from a network of pipes that ran up from the spotless quartz flooring.

The aeroponic garden was a popular place for students to take their ease. Even I found it a relief from the stark walls of the institution and the confinement of my own private quarters. It became my habit to venture there after lunch and before Maruyama's class.

I would wander amongst the greenery and hope that I would one day be able to observe the enchantments that pruned and pollinated the crops, that kept the elements off and the pests out and otherwise kept the garden in order. I was certain that the food we ate in the Refectory was grown here, but I had no idea who was responsible for harvesting the crops.

I was musing on such topics when I came upon Boudreaux, standing with two hands hooked through a low-hanging trellis and leaning forward, as if he was trying to drag the structure down on top of us.

"Hi," he said. I could tell he'd been waiting for me.

"Hello."

"I'm not sure anybody has mentioned this to you yet, but," Boudreaux canted his head so his smirk became a level smile, "you look awfully familiar."

"Do I?"

Boudreaux nodded. "I knew your father. We all knew your father."

I just stared at him.

"Your father was an asshole."

I shrugged. I knew that better than anyone.

Boudreaux let go of the trellis and drew himself upright. I had been threatened many times before, but never by someone so much smaller than me. "I didn't like your Pa, and I don't like you," he said. "You understand me, boy?"

"I understand everything about you."

Boudreaux raised a fist. He looked at it, looked at me. Opened his fingers. "You think I'm funny. Some little dick-cheese, acting tough. What am I gonna do, punch you in the kneecap?"

I'd faced enough bullies in my time to know how to deal with them. Stand your ground. Show no fear. Throw the first punch. "Perhaps if you stood on a box?"

Boudreaux closed his fist again and stepped away from me and began to speak. But he did not speak language; he uttered a sequence of hisses and glissandos.

Blows began to rain upon me before I could offer a response. Some blunt and invisible force struck me in the sternum, in the jaw, in the stomach, across the back of the head. I fell to my knees, gasping.

"Don't fuck with me, boy." Boudreaux did not even pause for breath. "This is the Academy. I don't need *size* to beat the shit out of you."

He walked away, humming tunelessly like a child making noise to amuse himself. I threw up.

When the retching stopped, I wiped my mouth and rolled onto my back. I looked up at the crops hanging above, bound to their trellises, magically maintained for some unnatural harvest. I wondered if any of them ever fell. I wondered if there was some process to sweep up such fallen specimens and dispose of them, or whether they were simply left to rot.

When Saad saw me limp into the Refectory, he picked up his tray and joined me at my table. I was angry that I had allowed this to become a habit.

"Are you okay, brother?"

"I'm not your brother."

"Friend, then."

I turned my attention to my meal instead of answering. When the meat and vegetables were all gone, I used the knife to cut the noodles into pieces I could pick up with the spoon. It wasn't the most elegant way to eat, but it was the best I could manage with the tools I had mastered.

Saad held his chopsticks above his bowl. Noodles reached up out of it and twined around the utensils. "You don't look well, friend."

"I'm fine." I searched in my bowl for more food, but there were only the tiniest of scraps sticking to the rim. I was still hungry.

"You're bleeding."

I touched my right temple. It came away red. "Everybody bleeds," I replied.

"Will you tell me what happened?" he asked.

Saad peered inside his bowl and twirled his chopsticks through its contents while he spoke. "The other American?"

I nodded.

Saad raised the chopsticks to his mouth. The noodles coiled around them swung up into his mouth, and he began to chew. "I told you to stay away from him."

I scraped my spoon over the sides of the bowl and inspected the greasy sheen. "He came at me."

Saad nodded. "He wants everyone to know who's the strongest. Especially you, coming from...where you came from."

I put down the fork and started spooning the flavorless broth into my mouth. Greasy hot water.

"He'll come at you again," said Saad. "At some random time. Just to keep you off balance. To reinforce your fear."

"I will be ready next time."

"Will you?" said Saad. "Do you think you can beat him, Art for Art?"

"I don't know. But I will be ready for him."

"Or perhaps you're thinking of setting an ambush. Surprise him, teach him a lesson."

I had considered the idea, but decided against it. An ambush would make it personal. I didn't care for petty revenge. "I am no teacher," I replied.

"How are you going to fight him? With your laundry charm? Or have you learned some new techniques from all your other friends?"

I just looked at him. "Do you have any such techniques?" I asked. "Could you stop him? Could any of *your* friends?"

Saad shook his head. "Me? No. Not yet. I cannot speak for my friends."

My bowl was now completely empty. I put down the spoon. "Then do not speak for me, either."

My frustration with the classes continued to grow. In the following weeks I found little new insight into the Art, and nobody was willing to trade techniques with me. I had nothing to offer them in return. I was sure there was a better way to learn, but Thieu was the only one teaching.

At the end of yet another of his interminable lectures I raised my hand.

"Ah, the questioner has more questions. Yes, Acolyte?"

"Is there somewhere in this building that I can study, Professor?"

"You have your own room."

Arakne sniggered conspicuously. She was sitting next to Saad. She had been watching him for weeks, moving closer and closer during class. Now she seemed to be in his presence constantly. Saad put his hand on Arakne's knee and shushed her.

"No, Professor," I replied, "that's not what I mean. Is there a library?"

"A library?" Thieu was astounded that I would ask such a question.

"A place with books."

"Acolyte, do you really think there is a place where the most valuable secrets of the unnatural world are recorded in books that anyone might freely borrow?"

"Yes," I said.

"Then you are more foolish than you look," Thieu replied. "Here at the Academy, we teach the Naming Art. True Names are the most valuable knowledge in the world, and we do not share them lightly. We do not write them down. We do not put them in books. We do not perform them or decorate them with tinsel and colored lights. We do not speak them aloud unless our intent in so doing is to destroy the object to which the name is attached."

I remembered how the Chancellor had named my father before he fell. I had felt something of it myself—from proximity or because we shared a name, I did not know. I had felt it, but only now was I beginning to understand what it meant.

"The naming art is one you must learn to perform in your own head, else your enemies will turn it against you."

I did not think this was a reasonable approach to education, but I could see the logic of it. Better still, it showed me that, powerful as he was, Boudreaux had a weakness. Powerful as he was, the glossolalia that accompanied his working showed that he was lacking the discipline.

But regardless of any shortcuts he had taken, he was still a long way ahead of me.

Saad and Arakne were sitting together in the Refectory when I entered. I chose a table far enough away that I wouldn't have to communicate with them, but from which I could continue to observe them—and Boudreaux. I was wary of friends and enemies, alike.

Saad waited until I was halfway through my meal before he got up and came to join me. Arakne did not accompany him.

"Hello, friend."

I gave him a peremptory nod and continued to slurp down my lunch. I no longer bothered to cut up the noodles. I had watched the other students eat and this seemed to be the correct way to go about it.

"Enjoying the food?"

I shrugged. "I've had worse."

"If you like, I will teach you a cantrip to spice it up. Salt and pepper. Herbs and spices."

"I have nothing left to trade, and well you know it."

"My gift to you," said Saad.

"Such a gift is always accompanied by a debt," I replied. The truth was that I did not much care how food tasted. It was fuel, and that was all.

"You slight me," he said. "I offer you this purely out of friendship."

"You told me that friendship has no worth here."

"I was exaggerating. Of course friendship has value."

"Way I see it, friendship is a just another kind of debt. I don't need your friendship any more than I need condiments."

"What do you need, then?"

"Information," I said. "Power. A way to defeat my enemy."

Saad's smile flickered. "That will be expensive indeed."

"And so we return to the start of our conversation."

Saad looked conspicuously around the Refectory. I had already scanned it, so I knew that Boudreaux and his gang had left. Arakne sat alone at the table Saad had abandoned, watching us from across the room with eyes that shone like reflectors. Saad nodded to her, and she approached. She did not bring her tray.

Arakne sat down beside Saad. She did not greet me.

"Tell our friend what you heard."

Arakne looked at me slowly. "The professor told you that there are no books here, and that nothing is committed to permanent record. But this is untrue."

I met her reflector gaze. "Go on."

"The Chancellor keeps in his office a book of names. The names of all the students who study here, or ever did."

A book of names. I already had a headful of names, but I had no idea how I had acquired them. I had no idea if they were accurate, and the stakes were too high for me to build any kind of stratagem upon them. If I could see that book–just a glimpse of it open might be enough–it would confirm for me if the names I knew were true, or if they were just a product of my imagination.

"How do you know this?" I asked.

"I have seen it myself," said Arakne.

"What were you doing in his office?"

"That's my business," she snapped.

"Could you find your way back there?"

"I don't know," said Arakne. "I have only been there once, in answer to direct summons. I do not think the Way is easy to find without his personal guidance."

"You'd dare to break into the Chancellor's sanctum?" Saad seemed more curious than alarmed. Curious to see if I could be provoked into it. "If you get caught, you'll be expelled, or worse."

"Who said anything about breaking in?"

I sat near Boudreaux in Maruyama's class. The next day I sat amongst his retinue, in Thieu's lecture. I followed them to the Refectory afterward and sat at a table close enough to them that I could overhear their conversation.

But there wasn't much to be heard. My presence was making them uncomfortable, and after they forced a few too-loud jibes about the welts on my face, the guffaws faltered and they sat around muttering.

Saad and Arakne watched, puzzled, from across the room. I paid them no heed. Even if I wanted their help, there was nothing they could do to aid me in this.

Eventually Boudreaux picked up his tray and slammed it down on the table, clattering the crockery and causing a general disturbance. "You're ruining my meal, boy," he said to me.

"I haven't done anything."

He got up, walked slowly around the table, and came to stand across from me. He was taller than me when I was seated, but not by much.

"You been following me around like a wet fart," he said.

"We have the same classes, and we dine in the same hall," I replied. "That is hardly my fault."

"Don't be smart with me, boy. Tell me what you're doing, or you'll get another beating."

I raised my head. "You beat me before," I said. "I respect that."

"So now you're following me around? I'd have thought you'd want to lie low."

"I'll never learn to fight if I hide from my enemies."

"You think I'm your enemy?" said Boudreaux. He pulled up a chair and sat in it. "You don't know shit about shit, boy."

"Enemy or not, you found cause to fight me."

"Fight?" said Boudreaux. "That wasn't any kind of a fight. It was a straight up whipping."

I nodded my assent. "That is true. I have much to learn."

"What do you think you can learn just from hanging around me?"

"I have no better ideas."

Boudreaux chewed the insides of his cheeks. "I could teach you some things," he said. "But you'd owe me."

"What do you want?"

"I want a servant. I want the great fallen professor's son to fetch my meals, clean my boots, wipe my ass. You do what I say, I'll protect you and I'll teach you to look after yourself. Maybe."

I stared at him flatly. "Let me make you a counter-offer."

Boudreaux raised a single eyebrow. "This ought to be good."

I stood up and spat in his eye. He staggered back off his chair, and I turned over the long trestle table, sending him scrambling away. I vaulted over it and went after him. I was bigger and I caught him inside with a couple of steps. I managed to land one kick before Boudreaux's goons seized me by the arms.

Boudreaux got up, one hand pressed to his cheek, hissing and spitting the liquid sounds of his magic through swollen lips.

I hoped he would not kill me this time when the blows began to fall.

I don't know how long it lasted, but I believe it was over quickly. I lost consciousness for a short time, and I have a woozy memory of Saad and Arakne pulling me clear while Boudreaux, bent over from exhaustion, gasped epithets at me.

Once I had recovered myself, I managed to shake them off, but by then they had delivered me to Sensei Maruyama at the sick bay.

She dismissed them with a look and sat me down on an adjustable bed. Here, finally, was a room that looked as though it belonged in a normal school. It contained cupboards and faucets and a sink and chairs and a desk.

Maruyama treated me with an ordinary first aid kit in a plastic box with a red cross on the lid. She cleaned my wounds with disinfectant, bandaged a cut on my arm, shone a light in my eyes, took my blood pressure.

"There's nothing broken," she said at last. "You may have a slight concussion, but you will live."

"Thank you, Sensei."

She sat looking at me, expressionless, as if waiting for me to say something more.

"Are you going to reprimand me?"

"I am not your parent," she said. There was nothing she could have said that would have made me more uncomfortable. "So long as you do not disrupt my classes, it is not my place to discipline you, or any other."

"Whose place is it, then? The Chancellor's?" Was I being too obvious? I resolved to say no more.

"I cannot speak for the Chancellor," said Maruyama, "But you need not fear. If he has words for you, he will make them known."

The Chancellor's summons was a subtle one. An idea that he wanted to see me. That I should go right away. There was no voice, no image. There was no avatar to deliver it. Just the idea that I should go. It was all that was necessary to send me limping through the halls.

This was my chance to discover the location of the Chancellor's rooms and see for myself what treasures they contained. One eye was swollen shut, but I would make do with what I had.

Before long, I understood why Arakne's description of the way had been so vague. For all the uniformity of the hallways I traversed, I knew that there was something different about them.

Perhaps the height of the ceiling was different, or the distance between the doors, the size of the tiles on the floor, the thickness of the doorframes. These hallways seemed to be just a little bigger than the others. The angles looked straighter. They were cleaner, although I had never observed the other parts of the Academy to be dirty. I was uncertain where I had turned to enter this new section of the building, although I had been paying close attention.

There was nothing to indicate which door led to the Chancellor's office, but I knew immediately which one to open. It wasn't locked.

The first thing I noticed about the room was the window. There was no window frame, just a glass pane that replaced the entire wall behind the desk. The view outside was of sky that was blue above clouds that were gray and gold and pink. Perhaps, if I pressed my nose to the glass, it would be possible to see the slopes of the mountain below, but from where I stood, only the firmament was visible.

The remaining walls of the room were concealed by bookshelves. If this wasn't a library, it was most certainly a surfeit of books.

Books. Bound in leather and brass. Row after row. There were no titles on the spines, only numbers, although they were not arranged in numerical order.

The Chancellor himself sat behind a huge mahogany desk. The only thing upon it was a single massive tome. The Book of Names that Arakne had described. It came to me that this was just the latest volume; that all of the volumes lining the walls were earlier volumes of the same, singular work. I coveted that book as I had never coveted anything before. It lay open before the Chancellor.

The pages were yellowed and dog-eared and ancient, covered with columns of text that would not resolve to my vision no matter how directly or indirectly I looked at them.

The Chancellor watched me squinting at the pages and smiled. I lifted my gaze from the swimming text up to meet his own. If anything, that was even harder to look upon. I was beginning to feel nauseous. Perhaps I really was suffering from a concussion.

"Thank you for coming to see me, Acolyte."

I stood before him with my hands at my side. He had not offered me a seat. There was no guest chair. "Chancellor."

"Acolyte, I hear that you have been fighting with another boy." The Chancellor's lips and jaw moved, but the rest of his face was completely still when he spoke.

"He struck first," I replied. "Punish me if you will. I was defending myself."

The Chancellor shook his head. "There is no rule against fighting in this Academy," he said. "If you have a disagreement with another student, you are free to pursue it to whatever end you see fit. No Faculty will intervene."

"To whatever end? What if one of us dies?"

"Students die here all the time, Acolyte. Some of old age, some of failure, some of loneliness...and some by violence."

"Then why have you brought me here?"

"You, acolyte, are a special case. Your father had many enemies here, and you have inherited them, whether you know it or not."

"There's nothing I can do about that," I replied.

"There is not," replied the Chancellor, "but engaging in a feud with students more powerful than you will only make it worse."

"He came at me first," I replied.

"You must find some peace with him," said the Chancellor. "And with the rest of the Academy. I cannot favor you over your peers, and I will not protect you."

I looked again at the pages of the Book of Names, but I still could not recognize a single character anywhere on its open pages.

"Be prudent," said the Chancellor. "Take no undue risks. You are a smart and talented boy. You will find your place here, if you are patient."

If I was patient.

If I lived long enough.

Act 4.

THE LIBRARY
— OF SHADOWS —

I spent the next two days wandering the halls, trying to find the Way to the Chancellor's office. I had no plan to burglarize it yet–I still needed to work out why I couldn't read the book–but I wanted to make sure that I did not forget how to get there in the meantime.

But I could find nothing. The corridors led to where they always had. There was no area where the dimensions of the walls looked different.

I walked outside of the ziggurat and could find no sign of the Chancellor's window glass–or any glass, for that matter. Even the colonnaded windows of the classrooms were open to the air.

I was thinking about scaling the walls when Saad came to me.

"I haven't seen you for a while," he said. "Is everything ok?"

I hadn't been back to class–neither Professor Thieu's nor Sensei Maruyama's–since my altercation with Boudreaux. "I'm fine," I said. My injuries were mostly healed already.

Saad sat down on the white marble steps. "Did you see the Chancellor's office?"

I was annoyed that he had figured out my plan, although I knew it was crude. "Yes."

"And?"

"I don't think I can find it again."

"So Arakne was right."

I nodded. It had not occurred to me to wonder why Arakne had been there, despite the way she had earlier dismissed my question. I should have inquired further, but at the time I had no concern for what she was doing.

"I will have to find something else," I said. "Some other source of knowledge and power."

We were alone on the steps. The sun was high above, and there was nobody in sight but our own two shadows, lying puddled at our feet.

"What if I told you there *is* a library?" he said.

"The professor says there is no such place in the Academy."

"It's not really a part of the school," said Saad, "but, if what I have heard is true, we might still be able to access it from here."

"Is there a library, or is there not?"

"There is...sometimes."

This felt like a trap. "How do you know?"

Saad hesitated. "The professor alluded to it."

I shook my head. "When? He only ever teaches the same lesson, over and over again."

A longer hesitation. "The...previous...professor. And it was not a lesson—it was a private conversation."

I just stared at him. It was the first indication I had that Saad had some kind of an affinity with my father. I did not know how to feel about this. Whatever he had taught Saad was certainly more than he had taught me.

Saad put his feet out in front of him and put his hands behind his head. "Have you heard of dark matter?"

"Dark matter is mass that mathematicians insist must exist, but which astronomers have failed to observe."

"Correct. Its existence, and perhaps even its very nature, must be inferred by its context."

"By the shadow it casts."

"There is a kind of Art based upon this," said Saad. "Upon the play of shadows." His face grew suddenly, strangely serious. "Literally, we are talking about the dark arts."

Now he had my attention. "Art is art," I said. "Are these shadow arts truly different from the Academy's discipline?"

"The Academy's teachings are founded upon the idea that names are...keys...that can be used to unlock all of one's secrets." He smiled when he said the word "key," but I did not react. "But there are other ways of identifying people."

"Fingerprints," I replied. "DNA."

"Yes," said Saad. "Any of those will do, if you have a sample from the source to match the trace. But there is still another way. No entity is entirely self-contained. Nothing with any meaning–no person or object or concept–can exist without context."

I was going to have to find out who was coaching Saad. "Unless you are a solipsist."

"If you are a solipsist, what interest does this discussion hold for you in the first place? If you really want to find something hidden, you must understand the context in which it exists."

"Are you ready to tell me about this library, or not?"

Saad was smiling once more. "It is said that even the most secret arts are codified and recorded in a place called the Biblioteca Tenebrae. The Library of Shadows."

"Have you been there?"

"Me?" Saad's confidence wavered. "No. It is a dangerous place, if the rumors are true. To my knowledge, there is nobody presently at the Academy who has dared to venture inside its halls. Not even the Chancellor."

"What about...the previous professor?"

"He never admitted it, but then, I never asked him directly. He was known as a man who was unafraid to travel. He was unafraid to take risks."

The Chancellor had told me to be patient and prudent, but whatever few virtues I possess, those are not among them. "Where is the entrance?"

Saad tilted his head and said, "According to the old professor? We need to find the place where shadows go at night."

I don't think Saad expected that I would want to go immediately and without further preparation. The Library of Shadows was a dangerous place, and I was willing to brave it with a laundry spell as my only resource. But that was, in fact, my best incentive.

How many more painful weeks and months and years would I otherwise have to spend in the Academy, bargaining for scraps of knowledge in the hope that I might eventually turn them into true power?

Besides, it was a library. However strange and dangerous it was, I felt that I would be in my element. I wanted to get into the Library of Shadows, and I wanted to do it soon.

It had been dark for hours when Saad knocked on my door. I did not have a watch; I had no way of judging how long I had waited.

I needed Saad because I had no source of light, and the halls were pitch black at night. I expected that he would have some kind of illumination spell that he wanted to show off, but once he arrived, I saw that he had a plain old battery-powered flashlight.

I don't know how long we walked the halls looking for the place, with Saad swinging the flashlight about and pretending that he knew where we were going, but I soon lost patience with him. He had no idea what he was doing.

"Give me that."

He made only a token protest when I took the flashlight.

I shone the light around experimentally. I turned it off; I turned it on. I aimed the beam at Saad and then at myself. I tried to make a strobe-light effect, but the torch had a twist-on head, which adjusted the brightness too gradually for that to work. Even so, it made the shadows roil about us. I was beginning to understand.

"You're wasting the battery," said Saad.

"Quiet. I know what to do."

I held the torch behind me and pointed it at my back, so that my shadow was cast before me. But I was too close to it; my shadow was huge. I needed a more distinct silhouette.

I gave the torch back to Saad. "Follow me," I told him. "Two meters' distance. Keep the torch on me."

"Why?"

"We need to go where shadows lead."

At first my shadow walked ahead of me, mimicking me precisely and in perfect time. Then, as we came to a junction, I thought its head indicated to the left. Maybe. I went left, and Saad followed as I had bidden him.

At the next corner, my shadow's head and shoulders angled right.

Saad was lagging. "Two meters." It took an effort of will to refrain from calling Saad by the name I had given him. "Keep up."

Around the next corner, my shadow lengthened its stride. I matched it as it stepped into a jog. We turned left at the next corner and my shadow started to lope ahead, lengthening as it got away from us. I sprinted to catch up and then match its speed. Saad's footfalls hammered behind me. I could hear him cursing through his ragged breath. The shadow bounced crazily off the walls as Saad struggled to aim the flashlight as he ran.

The beam flickered off me for just a moment. I caught a glimpse, in that brief interval, of my shadow leaping ahead of us, slewing around the next junction and vanishing from sight. I stopped dead. When Saad put the flashlight back to me, I cast no shadow.

"Oh shit." The torch trembled in Saad's hand. He did not know whether to keep shining it on me or to turn it away.

"Come on."

I turned the corner into darkness.

———◄●►———

I couldn't tell exactly where the corridor became a courtyard, but fifteen meters away from me, right there inside the Academy's walls and beneath its roof, there loomed a building that seemed bigger than the space that contained it–and the Academy was not a small place.

Darkness prevented me from judging the true extent of the Library, but this was no trick of poor visibility and curving sight lines, of parallax and false light. Though it was physically impossible, the Library had manifested inside the Academy.

The Library of Shadows was a massive gothic building. Clouds of liquid black bled from its every opening, hanging in the air like ink in water. Its huge doors stood open, but there was nothing but darkness visible inside.

A guardian stood between me and the entrance, a massive being as elaborately carved as the façade of the Library. Its armor was ribbed and scaled and spiked. A helmet concealed all of its face above its moustache, which drooped down over a considerable chin. I could not see its eyes, and I could not tell if the horns were part of its helmet or its head. It carried a scimitar that was almost as long as I was tall.

When I stepped forward, my shadow flowed across the floor to re-join itself to me. I had felt no loss for its absence, but it was good to be reunited with it.

Saad began to back away. "I'll, uh, just leave you to it, then," he said.

I could see the whites of his eyes. "Go on," I said. He fled.

—c●ɔ—

I approached the guardian slowly, holding my hands out and open in a placating manner. "I need to enter the Library."

"Then you will die," replied the guardian. There was no threat in its voice.

"Are you going to kill me?"

"Only if you challenge me."

I had no desire to fight the guardian. I was a thirteen-year-old child with barely enough magic to polish its boots. I hoped to find some way of tricking it or distracting it, but in the meantime it did not seem aggressive.

Since the guardian seemed willing to answer questions, if they were put to it in a peaceable way, I decided there was no harm in the asking. "If you're not going to kill me, then how am I to die?"

"The Library itself will kill you."

"Then why are you guarding it?"

"I do not guard the Library."

I looked through the doors behind the guardian. The darkness inside the Library was completely opaque. I wished I had taken the flashlight from Saad.

"Then what is it that you are protecting?"

"I protect those who enter."

"Because the Library will kill anybody who ventures inside?" I was on the verge of understanding.

"Any *body*, aye. This Library is not for bodies."

"Then who is it for?"

"The Library is for shadows."

I stared up at it for a long while before I understood. "And you will protect my body...while my shadow is inside."

"Yes, if you choose to engage my services."

"How do I do that?"

"You must ask me."

"And inside? Is it really dangerous, if I send my... shadow...in there?"

"It is a library. Your safety depends on what you read while you are within its walls and how you behave. I cannot protect you from the knowledge you seek, or from other readers whom you may somehow offend."

"Sounds fair."

The guardian regarded me in silence. It was not one for repeating itself, or for stating the obvious. It had no taste for small talk or gossip. Already I liked it better than everybody else I had met in the halls of the Academy.

"What else should I know?"

"There is no way to judge the time you are among the stacks. What seems like an evening's study may cost years of your life."

"All right," I said. I was not concerned about the price. I was young–years were the only currency I had. "Please protect me. I'm going in."

"As you wish," said the guardian.

I closed my eyes and extended my hands, keeping them at waist height with my palms pointed down. My shadow stretched across the floor toward the doorway. It stepped free of me once again, only this time my consciousness went with it. The guardian threw my inert body over its shoulder and stood aside.

I bowed my thanks, for I found that my shadow-self had no voice to speak them, and stepped through into the darkness.

In the Library of Shadows there is no architecture beyond the books and the shelves they rest upon. There is no ceiling, there is no floor. There is no horizon. There are just the stacks, aisle after aisle, extending away in every direction, rising to infinite heights, descending to infinite depths.

There is no perspective in the library. There is light, of a sort: ambient and unflickering, without direction and without source. Nothing casts a shadow, but the light itself is dark and without color. It is not truly light; it is a corona of information.

I rose up through the stacks, a thread of consciousness twisted through a skein of darkness.

Other shadows browsed amongst the shelves. Some of the Readers looked human, in the same abstract and unconstrained way that I did. Some of them did not. Some of them had no shape at all. During my first visit to the Library, I paid them little heed but to avoid them. Seldom, though, did I cross paths with any of them. The books they sought were far more rarefied than the ones that held my attention then.

Even now I do not know who authored the tomes in the Library. Are the texts literal books, or just psychic distillations of the knowledge and experiences of other beings once extant in the physical world? I do not believe the question can be answered. The Library is a metaphorical place, and no metaphor matches perfectly to the reality it describes.

But I had little concern for the scenery. Metaphorical or otherwise, the Library is a place filled with books. No matter their provenance, books are the most wonderful things in the world.

It is difficult to reckon the passing of time in the Library of Shadows, but I had not been there long before the Librarian found me.

The Librarian was made of shadow, like everything else in the Library, but it was a darker black than everything else, and harder-edged, as though it had been projected into the library from some external plane. It had no face, no head, no eyes—but I knew immediately that it was looking at me.

~You have returned.

The Librarian did not speak or sign. Hearing its voice was more like reading than listening, although there was nothing visual about the sense by which I perceived its words.

~I have never been here before.

~I know you. You have been here. You are Quay.

I was alarmed that it knew my name, and that it had named me with it. At the Academy, that would have been a grievous stroke, but here in the Library of Shadows it was only a label. A catalogue entry.

~I have never been here before.

Part of the Librarian's darkness washed over me. I felt no sensation, but I was pinned and helpless beneath it. After moments it released me.

~Ah. I had thought you were...smaller...than I recalled. A shadow cast from a steeper angle.

All at once, I understood.

~My father. My father was here.

~Your father. Your former self.

~Did he stay for long?

~He did not.

~Why not?

~He did not find what he was seeking.

~And what was he seeking?

~He was seeking names, of course.

~The names of his enemies?

~The names of everyone he knew.

It took time for me to process the enormity of it.

~Did he find what he sought?

~No. This library is a place of knowledge. It is not a census bureau.

~And yet you know my name.

~I am the Librarian. It is my job to identify the Readers who visit here.

~And to assist them?

~My assistance extends only to the collection. What is it that you seek here?

~I seek knowledge of the naming Arts.

~You will find that here, and more besides. But you will need other knowledge, which is not to be found in any book.

~Then how may I find it?

~You must look within yourself–or find someone else who can do it for you.

Now I was angry. I had not come to the Library for New Age platitudes.

~I know what is inside me. Meat and blood and bone.

The Librarian's shadow narrowed, as though it were turning in profile. It became a blade, then an edge, then a line.

~If you are to find the fate you desire, you will have to consider more deeply than that, Mr. Quay.

The Librarian narrowed to a single dark ray and then rotated out of sight, leaving me troubled amongst the infinite stacks.

By most definitions of the word, I am a monster, but I do not consider myself to be an evil man. I believe that few people are truly evil, and I believe there are fewer yet that might be judged as truly good.

I know that I lack many qualities that most people exhibit. I care little for the thoughts or feelings of others. I cannot truly appreciate beauty, and I have no taste for fine art or music or culture. I have no capacity for humor whatsoever. But these qualities are minor traits amongst those that make us human.

I share all of the vices that truly define our species. I am prideful. I am ambitious. I am selfish.

My only true concern is for power. I freely admit this.

I have taken no pleasure in hurting others, but power is meaningless if it cannot be demonstrated. When you have power, there is always a justification for such demonstration. This, then, is what sets me apart from other people: I have the capacity to do what they fear to do themselves.

I have found within myself the power and the talent to express my will, and the fortitude to stand against those who would destroy me for it.

I found all of these things in the Library of Shadows.

Act 5.

— SHADOWS CAST —

When I emerged from the Library, even the pre-dawn light, filtered through the Academy's windowless rooms, hurt my eyes. I blinked and covered them with my hand. I could not recall ever having felt so ill.

"How long?" I asked. My voice was deeper than I recalled, but it rang clear despite its lack of recent use.

"Two years, sixty-three days," replied the guardian. It seemed smaller than I remembered, though it was still huge. It took me moments to realize that I had grown.

I was sixteen now. My voice had broken. My hair was longer, but still constrained in its ponytail. I had no beard and supposed that I never would. I had never known my father to shave.

I was surprised to find that my clothing had grown to match my increased size. It was the same clothing I had worn since I left Brooklyn, with the same patches and fraying hems. Even my shoes still fit. The guardian had not shirked in its duty.

I felt strange in that new body. I felt powerful.

I named a light into existence, and the hallways of the Academy took form around me.

At first, I thought I was lost. When Saad and I had chased my shadow through the halls, we had not found the Library until I abandoned my sense of direction. But after the first corner, I knew exactly where I was. My room was four turns away, and I found it without error.

It was empty, as I had left it. I named a lock upon the door and lay down to sleep on the bare marble floor. I now had sufficient Art that I could have conjured myself a mattress, if I had so desired. I did not.

All I desired was sleep.

When I rose from slumber the next day, it was well past breakfast time. But I was not hungry. Lacking anything better to do, I decided to go to class.

Professor Thieu's classroom had not changed, and neither had the professor, but the students had aged - just as I had. They had also become a lot more peculiar. Outlandish fashions seemed the rule rather than the exception. Shape changing was fashionable, too—or at least the semblance of it. Some of my peers had grown horns, or extra arms, or tentacles, or wings. Most of these modifications were only illusions, but some of them really had altered their bodies.

I did not see any new students. I did not know if that was because none had been recruited, or if each cohort was allocated to its own classes. I had seen no evidence of any formal structuring of the school population besides the division between students and faculty.

My classmates were clustered in new groups, gossiping and bragging and preening. The air was thick with spell-craft: tiny dragons, butterflies, fireballs, arcs of lightning, flowers. A lot of smoke.

These students were not the listless bunch I had left behind. They were confident and powerful, smug little savants who thought they would one day own the world. I did not like or understand them. I didn't want to. The only things I wanted were located here in the Academy. I wanted the Mysteries for no other purpose than to possess them. I wanted them because they had been denied to my father.

In the classroom, Saad was still the only one actually listening to the professor. His suit was a newer and more expensive one than he had worn two years prior, and he was taller. He still walked on bare feet.

Arakne was leaning against him. She had matured, too: she looked more angular than before, and there was something strange about her joints. She had grown a cluster of secondary eyes in each of her sockets. These changes were real, biological adjustments. I wondered if they were practical.

Boudreaux stood at the back of the room. He had grown, but he was still one of the smallest in the class. His gang had grown as well. They squatted around him like toadstools, hunched to make him seem taller.

At first my peers were all too self-absorbed to notice me entering the room. I moved inside quietly and waited in the shadows by the doorway. It seemed my rightful place.

Slowly a hush spread through the room. Conversations died and heads began to swivel.

Saad was the first to react. He broke into a grin and ran to embrace me. I prevented him by holding up one hand, palm out, but this did not seem to lessen his delight. "Well, purple my prana and call me Petunia. You're back."

I wanted to strike him. Instead, I shouldered past and stepped forward.

Professor Thieu was less pleased to see me. "Indeed, you are. Where have you been, Acolyte?"

Arakne took a sideways step to the edge of my peripheral vision. I did not look at her, but I could see that she was working, spinning a web between the spread digits of both hands.

Thieu came to stand over me. "Well?"

I looked up at him and shrugged. "I have been studying."

"For the last two years?"

"Two years, sixty-three days."

Arakne spoke a name, and a thing like a tiny spider appeared in her web. She looked across at me, and so did the spider. I kept my eyes on Thieu.

"Perhaps you have indeed spent two years studying, Acolyte–but have you *learned* anything?"

"See for yourself." As I spoke, I drew a thin veil of polarized shadow over my face. The professor's chin multiplied as he drew it back to his neck.

Thinking me distracted, Arakne flicked her spider at my back. The construct was a subtle thing: just the barest shell of Art, a tiny amount of mass connected to its web by a filament so gossamer as to be invisible. A magical kick-me sign? A spy charm? I had no idea, but I didn't want it on me.

I made a tiny gesture with my left hand. It only took a minute effort to strip the construct of its name. The spider vanished, and Arakne turned away, wincing. She had been maintaining a live connection to it.

Thieu's lips twitched, and the illusion of darkness I had laid over my features flickered away. "A sun visor. Bravo, young mister..."

The pause at the end of his utterance was deliberate. Everyone in the room caught the significance of it. Most of them seemed startled. Saad only smiled.

"... young *Acolyte*. Keep it up."

The professor had stopped short, of course. To name me in front of the entire class would have been an act of uncalled for aggression. He just wanted me to recognize the threat.

The professor turned away, but the smirk remained plastered across his lips.

I knew then that I would one day have to destroy him. But in the meantime, I was hungry.

Saad joined me at my table in the Refectory, but I was in no mood to talk.

The food had not changed in the two years I had been gone, but the contents of Saad's bowl transmuted into a hamburger with fries in the interval between him putting down his tray and taking his seat. I failed to observe the working until after it was accomplished. Saad had grown subtler in my absence.

I could have changed my food, also. Or I could have simply made it appear that I had done so. I had the knowledge, but I did not want to waste the Art. I did not want to show my power. Not yet. Not unless I had to.

Destroying Arakne's spider in front of everyone had been a mistake. What harm could such a slight piece of Art have done me? I should have conserved my energy and waited until I could deal with it in private.

Arakne sat two tables away, where she could watch us with her dozen reflective eyes. She seemed worried–about Saad, I presumed, although he himself did not show any concern.

"So, you survived the Library of Shadows," he said.

"Was I not supposed to?"

"We...I knew you would."

I started in on the noodles with my knife and fork and spoon. The Library had not equipped me with the skill of using chopsticks.

"How was it in there, my friend?"

"Dark."

He nodded, thoughtful, as if I had provided him with some profound insight. "And? What did you see?"

"A whole lot of books."

"You'll have to show me around in there some time," he said.

"That's not how it works."

He took a moment to respond. Was I trying his patience, now, as he had earlier tried mine? No. Saad just nodded again. "Oh, I get it. Silence in the Library."

"More or less."

I did not want to explain that the concept of sound did not apply in there. All communication in the Library of Shadows must be written. Writing is language spilled dark upon the page.

I concentrated on my noodles while Saad nattered on. Gossip about the students, about the faculty. Boudreaux was growing stronger and controlled a bigger clique than ever–but they were bottom-of-the-class humps. I was not concerned with them. Saad had little to say about the Chancellor, or Thieu, or Maruyama. He did not mention Arakne, though she sat watching us with her many, many eyes for the duration of the meal.

When I finished my noodles, I got up and walked away, leaving Saad mid-sentence. Let him take my lack of courtesy however he wished–I had bigger problems. I had a very big problem indeed.

The Chancellor had named my father when he cast him down, and everyone at the school knew that I was his. That I bore the same name. Any of them could use it against me in the same way the

Chancellor had used it against my father. Any one of them could destroy me, and I was powerless to prevent it.

I did not know what else to do, so I went to Maruyama's afternoon lecture.

Thieu taught art and supernature; Maruyama science and reality. Thieu taught theory; Maruyama taught practice. Thieu taught dogma; Maruyama taught us how to solve problems.

"Welcome back, Acolyte," she said. I took my place on the left-hand side of the semicircle. There were even fewer students in her class than there had been when I first attended. "You have been away for a very long time."

"I have," I replied.

"Where have you been?"

"No place, really."

Maruyama's expression did not change. "All places are real, Acolyte," she said. "They may have different rules, and they may be difficult to access... but if you can travel to a place, it is somewhere real and true."

I inclined my head. Perhaps art and reality were less different than I had believed.

In Maruyama's lectures I discovered something like joy in mathematics and science. I liked grappling with problems that were abstract, but which could be solved by observation and analysis and logic.

"Without reason, we cannot discern what is natural from what is uncanny, what is true from what is false," Maruyama taught me. "Without reason we cannot appreciate the true nature of art or magic. Without reason there can be no Mystery to seek; there can be no mind or consciousness. Without reason there can be only unconstrained chaos and conflict," she said. "Without conflict there can be no mind, for the purpose of mind is to moderate conflict. The purpose of a mind is to reason; to impose order."

Sensei Maruyama might have put it more delicately, but in my experience, conflict is the natural state of the universe. Without it we are left with stasis and entropy. Without conflict, there can be no mind, and, thus, no reason.

As long as there is reason, there is reason for conflict.

Boudreaux was waiting for me outside Maruyama's class. He was not alone this time: his five toadstool cronies stood nearby, hunched and glowering. Boudreaux himself seemed to be in a good mood.

"Hello again," he said. "Long time, no see."

"Not long enough," I replied.

Saad appeared at the head of the corridor. He hesitated, then came toward us. I was unsure if he was coming to my aid, or if he just wanted to watch Boudreaux beat the tar out of me a third time.

"I'm hurt," said Boudreaux. "You went off on your trip and you didn't even say goodbye."

"Goodbye," I said, but I did not turn to leave. Two of Boudreaux's followers had taken up position behind me.

Boudreaux sighed, but the smirk never left his face. "You just gotta do everything the hard way, don't you, boy?"

I shrugged.

"It's the one thing I like about you," he said. "You take your medicine like a man."

Boudreaux started to mutter. The same hissing and harsh sounds he had spoken before. The attack this time was more complex and bore a heavier payload. I watched the power build and, when it was ready to unleash, I reached out and turned off one of the names.

The working collapsed in on itself. By the time Boudreaux knew what had happened, I had him by the throat.

"This is the third time we have had this discussion, and I have had enough of it," I said.

Boudreaux nodded and choked. Spit bubbled on his lips. His face was turning blue as he scrabbled to free himself from my grip.

Saad pushed his way through the toadstool gang, who seemed disinclined to come to Boudreaux's aid. "Wow, this is dramatic," he said. There was a smile on Saad's face, and I realized then that he and Boudreaux were enemies. Saad would profit from this as much as I would. More, probably.

I loosened my grip on Boudreaux's neck, but I did not release him.

"I think the young gentleman has learned his lesson," said Saad.

I knew that a single defeat would not be enough for him. He had beaten me twice before, and he was still probably the strongest practitioner in our cohort. I needed to put a definite end to his campaign.

"If I hear you speaking like that again I'll pull out your windpipe," I said. "You're not a child anymore. Keep your discipline in your head."

I released Boudreaux, and he doubled over, gasping, massaging his throat with his hands.

"This is your only warning," I said.

Boudreaux reeled away. His remaining minions closed ranks around him and dragged him off to safety.

The victory was mine, but I felt no relief. Boudreaux was someone I could understand and deal with, but I was beginning to see that I had bigger, subtler problems than that.

Saad clapped his arm around my shoulders. "Well played, my friend," he said, but I was no longer certain that I was, in fact, the player.

I continued to attend both Thieu's and Maruyama's classes. I learned little in the former and much in the latter, but the improvements to my Art came from the work I did on my own. Private study, meditation, practice.

Nobody spoke to me about my third altercation with Boudreaux, but word got around. Boudreaux kept his old position at the back of the class, but his circle of toadstools diminished quickly. He did not seem able to look in my direction anymore.

Saad was spending more and more time with Arakne. I ate alone in the Refectory. I did not miss his company.

Classes were like breaks in my real work–a chance to engage with the world outside of my own head; to stave off boredom while my subconscious continued to assimilate and refine my Art. My need for sleep diminished. In the dark hours I would sit alone in my room, turning the problems over and over, building my defenses.

I did my best work then, on the margins of dreaming, with my eyes open only to the night.

—◖●◗—

It was fully dark when they came to my room. Saad, Arakne, and a girl I had never seen before. She was tall and graceful, and she brought with her an exotic floral smell.

"Hi," said Saad. "Allow me to introduce our guest, Hana."

I must have looked shocked, because Arakne laughed. "Oh, it's not you, Hana," she said. "He's not really a people person."

I wasn't shocked that they had brought a strange girl to my room, at night, or even that they had been able to locate my sleeping quarters. I was shocked that Saad had identified the girl so openly. But it was just as well, because I could not think of a name for her, as I had for so many others at the Academy.

"Er, pleased to meet you," said Hana.

I did not reply, but I did shake her hand.

"Come on," said Saad. "We're going on an adventure."

I didn't move from my doorway.

Arakne crossed her arms. "I told you he'd balk."

"Come *on*," said Saad. "We need you with us."

"For what?"

"To show us the Way, of course."

I wasn't sure what he wanted, but I did like the fact that they needed me–that my presence was important to this undertaking. "Why should I?"

Saad met my gaze squarely for the first time in the months since I had returned from the Library of Shadows. "Because," he said, "what the fuck else have you got to do?"

"Study. Meditate. Sleep."

"You can study tomorrow, and for the rest of your life, if you want," said Arakne. "Tonight, we are going on an adventure, and you are going to come with us." She looked across at Hana, who just tilted her head and smiled.

The Academy was full of smilers, but they always seemed to be smiling at my expense. Hana's smile was sincere.

I suppressed a sigh. "What do you want to do?"

"Nothing too weird," said Arakne. "We want to go into the city and walk in the streets and eat a meal in a restaurant and enjoy each other's company. Like normal people do, every day, all over the world."

I did not enjoy the company of others. I had never desired to be one amongst the many. I had never wanted to be like them, or to be considered "normal."

"Normality" is a euphemism for "tedium," and I wanted no part of that. But I did want to travel, almost as much as I wanted power. And, suddenly, I wanted to spend time observing Hana's smile.

"Which city?" I asked.

"You know which city," Saad replied.

None of the customers in the Key in the Wall Ristorante Italiano were surprised to see the four of us emerge from the restrooms. Not even Arakne, with her spider eyes, drew undue attention. I was fairly certain this was Hana's doing. Something in the cloud of scent that enveloped her made us unremarkable. We pushed out onto the street.

New York City. Manhattan. It was a sunny day, but there was a cool wind to drive back the gritty summer humidity I remembered.

Saad turned to me. "This is your place," he said. "You lead."

It wasn't my place, not really. The two blocks surrounding my parents' house in Brooklyn was my territory. Manhattan and the other boroughs were places I went with my father, but I had never belonged there. Under my father's care, I had ridden the subways and walked the streets, but I had never been anywhere of my own volition—except for the time I had followed him.

"Where do you want to go?"

"Everywhere," breathed Hana.

Arakne just watched us with her compound eyes.

I showed them as much as they had stamina to see. Times Square, Radio City Music Hall, the Met, Central Park. The Upper East side, the Upper West, Broadway, Hell's Kitchen. When they had walked and seen all that they cared to, the group put a new request to me: pizza.

In my father's company we had never stopped anywhere unless it was a subway station. We had never stopped to eat, and the only place I knew by name was the Key in the Wall. I did not care to chance a meal there, but there was no shortage of pizza joints in Manhattan. I led the way into the first one I saw. It was a crowded, low-ceilinged place done up with fake brickwork and yellow lamps. The floor was linoleum, and the tables were '70s vintage Formica. We elbowed out some space and sat around a small circular table.

Hana sat to my left, Arakne on my right, and Saad sat across from me. I knew how it looked. Two couples out on the town. Arakne was clearly with Saad, which, by process of elimination, put Hana with me. It surprised me that I wanted her.

My body had grown during the years I had spent in the Library, and I was not yet comfortable with the new vantage it afforded me, much less the new needs and urges that came with puberty.

At the Academy I just focused on my studies, but here, in the city–in the real world–it was more difficult to ignore the new desires that my body imposed on me. After all that time spent bodiless, I did not trust it.

We ordered food. Saad ordered a bottle of wine. Although we were clearly underage, the waiter did not seem concerned. I knew that was Hana's doing, although I could not detect her working any Art.

There was a moment of silence following the waiter's departure. I turned to Hana and said, "Tell me who you are."

Saad looked surprised to hear me speak out of turn. Arakne broke out a grin that was unnaturally widened by a pair of mandibles, each as long as a finger.

Hana smiled. "As you know, my name is Hana. My Mistress and I have been guests at the Academy for the last week."

"In what capacity are you guests?" It was news to me that the Academy permitted visitors.

"It's a study program, of course. Some elements of the faculty are studying our workings, and we, in return, are studying yours."

"I haven't seen you around," I said.

"My Mistress has been in private consultation," said Hana. "It is my job to attend to her."

"And why aren't you attending to her now?"

"She allowed me some time off," said Hana. "I thought I would spend it with people my own age."

This did not explain how she had come to the company of Saad and Arakne, or what we were doing here so far from the Academy.

"Who is your Mistress?" My questioning was making Saad and Arakne uncomfortable, but Hana did not seem put out.

"You need not concern yourself with her," she replied. "She is very old and does not socialize with the likes of us. You will never meet her."

The wine arrived. Saad sniffed the cork like an expert, swished a mouthful around his palate. He nodded, and the waiter poured for all of us. The waiter seemed as impatient with the ritual as I was. This was not the sort of restaurant one chose for its wine list. Not one of us was older than seventeen and, whatever Art Hana had employed to bamboozle the waiter's senses, he must surely have known us for a gang of fools.

Saad grinned at my annoyance. He raised his glass and cleared his throat. "To our guest," he said, "Hana, the graceful flower."

We clinked glasses and drank the wine. I did not like the taste. It was sour and fruity, and it warmed my skin as I consumed it.

"Tell me about your Arts," I said to Hana.

Saad answered for her: "Hana practices a shamanic tradition." She gave him a look of mild annoyance.

"Is your school like ours?" said Arakne.

Hana shook her head. "We have no school," she said. "We have no governing body. Our arts are traditional, taught from mistress to student, and practiced within our own communities."

"You're witches," I said.

"We are shamans and witches and medicine men and faith healers. Our arts are very different from your Naming Art. They are much less direct."

"Hana and her colleagues work from inside natural systems," said Saad. "The Academy's discipline puts us outside of nature."

"Your arts transform," said Hana.

"And destroy," said Saad. "Hana's gifts are subtler: healing, communication, divination."

"You coerce," said Hana. "We persuade."

"Or deceive," I said.

"All of us practice deception," she replied. "Some better than others."

Some, like my father. That was the fundamental difference between him and me. My father had managed to deceive every soul he knew. I could deceive no one but myself.

"There are other schools, other disciplines, of course," said Saad. "Many of them. Summoners, topomancers, necromancers, elementalists. They are perhaps more numerous than we who study at the Academy, and more specialized in their arts."

"Don't worry," said Hana. "We lowlanders all know who has the biggest stick."

"Lowlanders?" I asked.

"Those of us who don't get to study up on the mountain," said Arakne. "Have you never heard the term before?"

I shook my head.

Saad poured more wine for everyone else. I hadn't touched mine since the first sip. I took another mouthful, but I renamed it water before I swallowed.

I looked again at Hana. "I am surprised the Chancellor has allowed anyone to visit the Academy."

"He doesn't like it," she replied. "He has made that abundantly clear."

"You know how he is," said Arakne. Her face was flushed from the alcohol, although the others seemed unaffected. Perhaps they had a tolerance.

Perhaps they, too, were altering the wine. "Always on about purity and corruption. He thinks that the Academy's way alone can reveal all the mysteries."

Saad shook his head. "The Chancellor is no fool," he said. "He is very old and very wise, and he knows that there are many ways to power. But he is the supreme master of our discipline, and he does not want those who study under him to learn arts he himself has not mastered."

He poured me another glass of wine. I ignored it. "Why, then, does he permit these visits?" I asked.

"Ah." Saad sipped from his glass. "The Chancellor does not exercise complete control over the Academy. The exchanges were instituted by...a former member of the faculty...and, even in his absence, he has his supporters."

All three of them fixed eyes on me, but I was suddenly too angry to speak. Everybody knew more about my father than I did, about the Academy and its faculty and its politics. Was that the purpose of this whole expedition? To find out what I knew? To win my allegiance to some political faction within the Academy?

The waiter returned with our pizzas and we each claimed slices. The others negotiated amongst themselves for parmesan cheese and chili flakes. I ate my share plain and in silence. Saad poured more wine for the others, but I let my glass remain full.

Eventually the conversation turned back to me.

"You know, it's very cool that you're from the city," said Hana.

"I'm from Brooklyn."

"It's all New York to the rest of us," she replied. "It's the center of the world. Especially if you're from where I am."

"Come now." Arakne spoke around a mouth full of pizza crust. "Everyone loves an Aussie, especially a talented one."

Hana shook her head. "The true Australians have their own arts," she said. "And their discipline is no closer to mine than it is to yours."

"One day, you will have to explain what that means," said Arakne, dabbing her mouth with a paper napkin.

"They keep their secrets close," said Hana. "Same as you."

Everyone looked at me again. I said nothing.

"Why are you angry?" asked Arakne. "Who are you angry with? Us? The Academy? Your father?"

Saad looked uncomfortable. "I thought we had agreed not to..."

"Don't be an idiot," said Arakne. "Everybody knows about his father. But the professor–the real professor, I mean–is gone now." She fixed on me with all those unblinking spider-eyes. "You know that you are among friends here, don't you?"

"So you say." I rose to my feet.

Saad stood up, too. "Look," he said. "I...we know it's hard, but you have to understand. He's a great man. A powerful man. A man of vision."

"He was," I replied.

"He was." There was sadness in Saad's voice, and a hint of shame.

"If we're done eating," I said, "it's time to pay the bill. I'm ready to go home."

The Chancellor was waiting for us when we returned to the Academy. It was not long before dawn. We had been away for more than 24 hours.

The Chancellor said nothing to us as we trooped out of the Door.

"Did we do something wrong, Chancellor?" Saad's smile was insolent.

"You have not broken any rules," he replied.

"Then why are you here?"

"It appears that somebody left a Door open on the threshold of my Academy," said the Chancellor. "It's getting a little draughty, and my bones are old." He turned away and started back up the stairs.

"Well, that was fun while it lasted," said Saad.

The Door to New York was closed. Sealed over, as if it had never been.

Now I had no way to go home.

Hana came alone to my room that night with a will-o'-the-wisp light burning above her cupped hand. She had a bundle under her free arm.

"My Mistress and I are leaving tomorrow."

"That was sudden," I replied.

"Our excursion to New York has provided the Chancellor with all the excuse he needed to terminate the study exchange." She pulled the door behind her.

"We broke no rules," I said.

Hana shrugged and smiled. "Security risk, he said. You showed a Way into the Academy to an outsider."

"You were already here," I said.

"By the Academy's grace," she replied. "You are lucky that no blame will fall on you."

"I did not make the Way. Nor did I set the Door."

"No, you didn't," she said. "That was your father's doing."

"I thought the Doors and Ways the provenance of the topomancers," I replied.

"Certainly. Do you not think that if your father was exchanging knowledge with my kind that he might have done the same with the travelers?"

I shrugged.

"Thank you for showing us the city," said Hana. "I hope one day to live there."

"I thought shamans were bound to their communities?"

"Shamans live outside the tribe," said Hana. "We can choose which communities to service. We can choose none at all, if we prefer it–although few of us do."

"And you?"

"I will choose my own people."

"But...your Mistress..."

"My Mistress is not my jailer. I'm free to serve her, or not, as I please."

I set the lock and then turned to examine the bare walls of my room.

Hana followed my gaze from wall to wall, down to the ceiling and up to the floor. "I love what you've done with the place."

I shrugged.

Hana cast the bundle in front of her. I stepped back, surprised, as it rolled open across the floor. She looked at me reprovingly. "Aren't *you* skittish?" she said. "It's only a blanket."

It was indeed a blanket: thick and woolen, checkered with blue and white squares. Two of the ends were fringed with blue tassels.

She took my hands and pulled me toward her. "Come here," she said. "We only have one night, and there's a lot I want to teach you."

———❮●❯———

The shaman's art is one of influence, but I did not need any encouragement or coercion. Say what you will about me, I was ever the willing student.

I told myself that what I felt in Hana's arms was only the satisfaction of a bodily need, but I knew there was more to it. It was a more complex emotion than I was then equipped to understand. The need for dominion was a part of it, of course. The need to possess. The need for affection was another component, if only in trace amounts. I liked Hana, but I felt no particular need to protect or cherish her.

But that was not all that Hana taught me. After our coupling–perhaps even during–she taught me some fraction of her own arts. I received them as hungrily as anything else that night.

I was not the only one with a hunger. Hana took what little I had to give, and she seemed grateful for it.

All the while I felt eyes upon us, although I had warded the room as best I could. I felt the presence of another, there in my bare little chamber. Though I could barely perceive it, I knew that it was a woman, and that she was as powerful as anyone I had met, save perhaps the Chancellor. Hana's Mistress.

But why was she spying on us? What secrets did she and Hana know about me, and why was I the only one from whom they were kept?

Act 6.

EINE KLEINE
— NACHTMUSIK —

Although Professor Thieu was the teacher of Art, it was Sensei Maruyama who taught us how to make the imagination real.

"Mind is the interface between art and reality," she said. "But a mind is much more than just that. A mind is a nexus of identity and memory and reasoning power and matter. Through the medium of the body, it can interact with the world around it. Indirected through material reality, minds can inform, influence, and deceive each other. That, Acolytes, is how art is created."

There were perhaps eight of us in the room. We sat, as always, arranged in a semicircle around her. I sat at the furthest extent of the arc on Maruyama's left; Boudreaux occupied the same place on her right. Saad and Arakne sat beside me. The other four I did not trouble myself over.

Boudreaux spoke up. "You say Art, but there are many kinds of art besides our own," he said. He had given me no trouble since our third and final altercation. He had abandoned his toadstool gang and reapplied himself to his studies. This new Boudreaux was quiet, except when he had a question for the teachers. This new Boudreaux was a lot like me.

"What I say is no less true for a painter, or a musician, or an actor," replied Maruyama. "However the final work is rendered, art is art."

Boudreaux was not yet willing to concede. "But... the practice differs..."

"Superficially, the practice differs with the medium," said Maruyama. "And, of course, with the artist. But what is meant by practice? How does an artist, in any medium, go about the creation of art?"

Arakne spoke up. "Art begins with a state of mind."

Maruyama nodded, or perhaps bowed, the affirmative. "Musicians and painters and mathematicians and shamans–all of them must find the place within themselves from whence the art will flow. Trivial works can be learned by rote or calculated on the fly, but more complex pieces require the raw processing power of the subconscious. The dreaming mind."

Maruyama waited, but nobody spoke into the silence, so she continued, "Being able to find and maintain such a dream state and still invoke one's conscious will is the true discipline of any artist or magician."

Her next question was addressed to Arakne. "Acolyte, do you know what sets the practitioner of the Arts apart from other humans?"

"The ability to impose our dreams upon the world."

"Correct. This is something all artists hold in common," said Maruyama. "The ability to make real their imagination, in a sustained and meaningful way. The conscious mind is attuned to negotiate with external reality. The artist must learn a mode of consciousness more suitable for dealing with that which is not."

I had learned some of this from Hana. At the heart of her art was the trance: the ability to dissociate the waking mind from its usual preoccupation with reality.

Boudreaux put up his hand. "Sensei, how can these mental states be cultivated?"

"There are as many ways to achieve this mental state as there are practitioners of the arts," replied Maruyama. "Some take drugs, or confine themselves to sweat lodges. Ascetics fast; hedonists indulge. Some try sleep deprivation; others try lucid dreaming. Some prefer solitary meditation, and others look to public performance.

"In my culture, we have the concept of *mushin*: the Zen teaching of no-mind. In a state of *mushin*, one does not concentrate on the task at hand. One does not focus on it. One opens all senses wide and lets all the information in, and then one acts accordingly."

I raised my hand. "How is it possible to act when one is receiving the information without having a mind to process it?"

"One does not consciously reason with the information," said Maruyama. "One allows any emotions roused to wash past in a rush of chemicals. They do not affect what one observes, what one must do. One must absorb the information and then act or react as one has conditioned oneself. This is the purpose of ritual."

"Ritual leads to superstition," said Boudreaux. "To imprecise thinking and flawed logic."

"Not if it is performed with proper understanding," said Maruyama. "Correctly executed, ritual trains the mind to correctly parameterize the work and deliver it to the subconscious for processing. The subconscious is vastly powerful, but it is not easy to harness. That requires long hours of practice, even for the most talented among us."

And how I practiced. All my days at the Academy, in all of my spare time, I practiced. I practiced the skills I had learned from other students, I practiced exercises I had learned in the Library of Shadows. I practiced the forms that Hana had taught me.

I did not practice the shadowmantic disciplines I had glimpsed in the Library, but I meditated long upon their workings. The better versed I became at the Academy's Naming discipline, the better I could feel the shape of those dark arts that reflected them.

There were many things to learn, and I set my days to the study of them. I knew that eventually my enemies would come for me, and I needed to be ready for them.

I knew that they, too, were preparing. No matter how strong I became, if I waited for them passively they would trap me and overwhelm me. I needed to act first, and before that I needed information about them.

I had been thinking a lot about the faction to which my father had belonged, and I began to suspect the nature of the secrets they had been keeping from me. One of their secrets, at least.

It was an avenue I did not wish to explore, but it was the only clue that I had.

———⊂●⊃———

Astral travel to places that are metaphorical, like the Library of Shadows, is relatively easy, but it took work before I could confidently send my awareness to real places.

The Academy, of course, is warded against such incursions, but also has a policy of monitoring any and all projections out of its grounds. I spent weeks studying the school's firewalls, testing them, breaking them, until I was confident that I could do what I needed, undetected.

This was exactly what my father had done. He had bastardized the Academy's teachings with foreign arts, and he had used those bastard forms to conceal what he was doing from those who would have prevented him.

My father had many more years to perfect the task than I. He had better access to the Academy's teachings, he was better trusted, and, though his methods were not acceptable to the Chancellor, his ambitions were ones the Academy expected and sanctioned. My own ambitions were nebulous and ill-formed. Mostly, I was just reacting to my environment. My truest purpose was to survive my father's legacy.

Through no fault of my own, the entire faculty knew my name. Sooner or later, they would use it to spear me back onto the world; to take my powers; to render all of my hard-won learning useless.

And so, I decided it was time to seek out my father.

I locked and sealed the door to my cell with every scrap of Art that I had available to me. If some enemy penetrated my room while my consciousness was away, I would be utterly vulnerable. I had received no uninvited visitors since Hana had come to me, but I could leave nothing to chance.

The working was easy. I found the trace, set the wards, and pushed straight up. The effect was immediate. I looked down from a cornice above the door to see myself sitting cross-legged with my hands open on my thighs. There was no light in the room, but since my astral self lacked eyes, it did not need light in order to see. I could see my shadow, too, cast at an impossible angle. I did not wonder how it could exist in darkness. Art is metaphor, and metaphor is a shadow of reality.

I drew myself through the ceiling, and my shadow followed, stretching up through the Academy's white stone walls. Up, up, until I was high above the grounds, high above the mountains. The clouds below were a churning sea of gray. The night sky above was unending and bright, set with the fires of a septillion visible stars.

I looked down to see my shadow racing up toward me, arms extended. It engulfed me, consumed me and all of those brilliant stars. I hung above the Academy, bound up in that darkness, blind and empty and invisible.

No wards contained me. No shields disrupted my projection. No alarms triggered. No members of the faculty came to intercept me. I was free to do as I pleased. I had slipped through the Academy's security like a shadow under the door.

I turned my eyeless gaze across the leagues and miles to my parents' house in Brooklyn and cast my shadow there.

It felt strange to be back in the house after all my time away. Even though I had never seen the place from my present vantage, the house did not look different. I felt at home.

In the living room, my mother was asleep on the sofa. There was a bottle of gin on the coffee table, and a full glass. I could see, now, the damage my father had inflicted upon her. I could see the enchantments with which he had bound her; the spells he had used to program her to maintain his secret works. *Protect the child. Tell no one the truth. Obey me without question.*

The bindings had failed when the Chancellor struck my father down, but by then the commands had become engrained in habit. My mother followed his orders still, with only a sliver of volition remaining to her.

Upstairs, on the second floor, the door to the master bedroom gaped open. I rose to it without use of the stairs and went through.

My father lay on the bed, propped up by a pillow, crowded by life support machinery. He was thinner than I had ever seen him. His hair was streaked with white, and now it hung loose to his shoulders. He looked foolish, lying there, open-mouthed, in his flannel pajamas. His eyes were closed.

I do not know who returned him to the house. Some ally at the Academy, no doubt. Perhaps even the Chancellor. Probably the Chancellor.

The record player stood amongst the ventilators and heart monitors beside the bed. A black disk turned beneath the needle.

My astral self possessed no senses besides the strange version of sight, so I couldn't hear the music–but I knew what was playing.

I watched from my high vantage as my shadow caught up with me, sliding in through the doorframe and spreading across the roof like a water stain from an overflowing gutter. Together, we spilled down the wall toward my father.

There was a breathing mask over his nose and mouth, so we went in through his eyes and ears.

First, there was music.

Now that I was inside my father's head, I could hear it through his own sensorium: transduced from vibrations to electrical impulses by the apparatus of his ears, coalesced into data by his brain and projected into music in the machinery of consciousness.

Mozart. My father's favorite. It was kind of my mother to keep it playing for him. It was kind of the Chancellor to allow him his hearing when he had shut down his other senses.

"Father," I said. My astral self had no form, no vocal cords, no tongue or lips. I projected the sound directly into his mind.

And there he was, far in the distance. My father, wearing his robes, with his black hair tied back. He was his old self, not the withered version I had seen on the ventilator. Even so, his posture was slumped; head down, eyes closed. He cast no shadow upon the ground, which took the appearance of a salt flat, extending from horizon to horizon. The sky above was a featureless expanse of black.

As I approached him, the cracks in the terrain drew together, curling into intricate loops and whorls. "Father."

He came to with surprise on his face. In the distance, lightning arced down to the cracked gray earth.

"Father, it's me."

He looked around, bewildered.

"Father. Can you hear me?"

A look came across his face that I had never seen before. It was the first time he had ever seemed glad of my presence.

"My...son."

I gathered my will and manifested an avatar for him to see. I showed him my true self, wearing an image of my current physical shape. Eighteen years old, in the same jeans and a black t-shirt I had worn the last time we were together. But I did not inhabit that avatar. I kept my vantage high above both figures.

I was as tall as he was, but he was still the bigger man, broader across the shoulders and chest. His robes billowed, although there was no wind.

"My son. You have grown powerful," he said. I could hear uncertainty in his voice. "Did the Academy take you in?"

I nodded. "Father, I am surrounded by enemies." The eyes in my avatar's skull were black. The shadow it cast extended all the way to the horizon.

My father touched a finger to his lips. "Of course you are. You are...my child."

"They will destroy me, Father. They are just waiting for the most opportune time."

"They will not destroy me, and they cannot destroy you." Lightning forked up from the ground and down from the sky. "Now they must contend with both of us."

He stepped toward me and extended a hand. "You will return to them, my son. I will lend you my power, and together we will crush them. I will be Chancellor, or you." His eyes never wavered from mine, though my gaze was black and empty. Even now, the only words he had for me were orders. "We will take the Mysteries for our own."

My avatar accepted the proffered hand.

"First, you must restore me to my flesh. Pay attention–I will show you how. You have the Art for it now. I can see that."

Electricity sparked between the whorls in the terrain. The darkness of the sky frayed, and cloudy light bubbled through the loosening weave. In preparation for the working that would re-embody him, he had opened the psychic shields that protected his core.

"Open yourself to me," he said, "as I have to you. I will show you what must be done."

He thought I was too young and foolish to understand that he was vulnerable. He thought me too naïve to recognize that he was lying. He was partly right. I knew he was vulnerable, but I did not yet understand the enormity of his true intentions.

A moment passed before my father sensed that something was wrong. "Do as I say, my son. Time is of the essence."

My lip curled. "No, Father. I don't think so."

He rocked back on his heels, shocked. I did not release his hand.

My father had never given me anything but his name and his enemies. He would never share anything with me in the future; I knew that for certain. If I freed him, he would take it all for his own and leave me with nothing.

"But...my son..."

"Now you have time for me, Father? After all these years? Now that I have power and you do not?"

"But, my son...I couldn't. It was forbidden."

"I know you broke the rules just by keeping me, but if you truly cared for me, you would not have treated me like an item of property."

"You were never my...property. I would no more harm you than I would myself."

"Even now you lie to me. You knew the Academy took me in. You know precisely my situation there. I do not know the extent to which your servants there have manipulated me, but I am certain they tell you everything."

A hesitation. "I needed you to grow strong..."

I let go of his hand. He pulled away, staggering to regain his balance as if I had shoved him. "If you needed that, you would have helped me instead of using my classmates against me. You say that you will share the Mysteries with me. Did you promise them also to Saad?"

He took a step away from me. "How did you learn...?"

"Perhaps I am less stupid than you think me," I replied. It was too late for him to stop me.

He held up his hands. "No. No, my son. My son. You misunderstand. Listen to me," he ordered. *"Listen* to me."

But I was done listening.

My father did not stir in his bed. The head injury incurred on the steps of the Academy had left him paralyzed. His intellect was intact, and some of his senses—hearing and, perhaps, touch—but that was all that remained to connect him to the outside world. His power was greatly diminished by this infirmity, for all Arts are founded on the ability to perceive.

It is difficult to affect the material world through a projection, as with the one I had sent to my father, but the working I needed only required a tiny amount of power. Just enough to burst a blood vessel in the afflicted part of his brain.

My father spasmed once and then fell limp one last time. It was a small aneurysm, carefully targeted. I did not think it would kill him, but it would cost him dear.

In my father's bedroom, the record continued to spin beneath its needle, but there was nobody left to hear it.

Act 7.

THE ENEMY OF MY
— ENEMY IS MY ENEMY —

I was sitting on the eastern terrace, practicing my discipline in the company of the rising sun, when Professor Thieu came looking for me.

I had my eyes open wide, but the brightness did not hurt them. I had covered them with a film of darkness. The sunlight could not harm me, though I allowed it to warm my skin.

Professor Thieu stood for minutes beneath the colonnaded archway, regarding me as he might a curl of feces found upon his pillowcase. My shadow was upon him, streamed long upon the ground and climbing the Academy's white marbled walls.

Thieu approached slowly. He came to a stop near to my right hand and stood there, squinting into the sun and waiting for me to acknowledge him. I did not.

"Acolyte," he said.

"Professor." I did not bother to turn my head.

"I haven't seen you in my class for a while."

"I have given up the hope that you will teach me anything of value."

"The Arts of power hold no interest for you, then?"

I turned to regard him with my black-lensed eyes. "They are my only interest."

He scowled but swallowed an angry reply. "I am concerned for you, Acolyte. You do not attend my classes. You do not socialize with the other students. You are in a...difficult...position here, through no fault of your own, and we, the faculty, are concerned about you."

"You, and the faculty, have a strange way of showing it, Professor."

"There are those of us who know who you really are, Acolyte. We know you, and we worry about the path you have chosen."

I stood up. "Let's not be coy, Professor," I replied. "I know my presence here complicates whatever strange and sinister plans you have concocted with my father."

Anger thickened his features. He blinked them back to passivity while I continued to speak.

"Your plans are of little concern to me. I seek the Mysteries, as do all the students here. I don't know what your agenda is, but I will not oppose you unless you think to involve me in it."

Thieu tucked his hands into the dagged sleeves of his robes and raised his chin. "The agenda is your father's," he replied. "And your presence here has a direct bearing upon it. You are involved, whether you like it or not."

"My father has been cast down and exiled," I replied. "I am not his game piece, and I will never be. If this causes you difficulty, I suggest you take it up with him."

Thieu's eyes widened, then narrowed. "So you know he's alive."

"I visited him just this week."

"And what did he say to you?"

"Ask him yourself. See if he can still hear you."

Thieu blinked again. Twice. Three times. His lips parted, but it was moments before he spoke. "What have you done, boy?"

I was used to condescension from my betters, but this was the first time an adult had ever shown me fear. I can't say I disliked it.

"What have *I* done?" I shrugged. "I am the innocent victim of his crimes, you may recall. I have taken steps to stop that from continuing."

"He's your *father*, Acolyte. Have you no sympathy for him? No care for his legacy?"

"His legacy has endangered my life. I have no more sympathy for his plight than he ever had for mine."

Thieu turned in a swirl of fabric and stalked out of the terrace.

I turned my eyes back to the sun and let my shadow blot him from my sight.

The Chancellor's summons came at night. Once again, I walked those strange halls, following only the faint tugging at my attention. Despite my growing mastery, I was immediately disoriented on the journey. The Chancellor effortlessly deceived the new senses I had come to rely upon, and I felt almost the same trepidation I had the first time he had called me, as a boy with neither power nor art.

"Thank you for coming to see me, Acolyte."

I stood before him with my hands at my sides. "Chancellor."

"Young man, I know you have had a difficult time at this Academy. You were enrolled here in unpleasant circumstances, and my decision to take you in was not a popular one with the rest of the faculty."

Through the glass behind the Chancellor, I could see the night sky. A sickle moon shone brightly, but gauzy clouds concealed the stars. Perhaps they had been masked out, to prevent anybody from navigating by them. Perhaps they did not exist in whatever sub-reality the Chancellor's rooms occupied.

"I have noticed."

"Your father's mistakes were his own, and I do not think you should suffer for them–but you have suffered, nonetheless."

"I can deal with it."

"I don't want you to 'deal with it.' I want you to understand the situation. I took you in because you have a rare talent, and because I could not leave you with your father."

"You are the one who struck him down." There was no accusation in my voice. We both knew his actions had been necessary.

"I struck him down, but I did not destroy him," said the Chancellor. "That was why I had to take you in. Do you understand me?"

I truly thought that I did.

"Perhaps you made a mistake," I said. "Perhaps you should have killed him."

"Perhaps I could have justified that. But Professor Quay had many...allies, if not friends...and it would have stirred up trouble."

Hearing my father's name–my name–spoken gave me a queasy feeling. I swallowed hard and said, "It would have been more expedient to destroy me than to take me in."

The Chancellor did not hesitate. "Yes. Your existence is your father's greatest transgression. You are the embodiment of the danger that he and his like pose to this Academy. Do you understand me?"

Every time he asked me if I understood I became a little more irritated, but something about the question disturbed me deeply. Was he just patronizing me, or was he actually trying to gauge my understanding of the situation? What connection had I missed?

"If you had destroyed him, you would have faced the wrath of his allies," I replied, "but by saving me, you have increased the disfavor of your own people."

The Chancellor clasped his hands and narrowed his eyes. "Have you chosen a side?"

I shook my head. "I have not, and I will not."

The Chancellor nodded. Perhaps he did have a neck, after all. "I am told that you are not good with people."

"I have never denied it."

"Perhaps that will be your salvation." He did not sound convinced.

"From whom do I need to be saved, Chancellor? From my father?"

The Chancellor shook his head, as if to counter the motion of his earlier nod. He looked down at the Book of Names, touched the pages with his gnarled fingers. Then he looked at me again. "No, Acolyte. Not from him. That is why I have called you here."

I folded my arms.

"There was a fire in Brooklyn last night. Your parents' house...the whole block...was consumed."

I understood immediately. "They were inside."

"They were. Both of your parents are dead."

"Are you certain?"

"Yes," said the Chancellor. "I am certain."

"This was no accident." I was surprised to find that I was angry about it. As my mother and I had once belonged to my father, I had come to feel that my parents now belonged to me. They were mine. This was an attack on my property. It was an attack directed at me.

"Listen to me, Acolyte," said the Chancellor, rising from his seat and putting his knuckles on the desk. "This is a tragedy, but it took place away from the Academy. I do not have the authority to police incidents that occur outside of these walls."

"My father's misdeeds took place outside of these walls, and you saw fit to bring him low."

"Your father's actions jeopardized the Academy and its precepts, and so I cast him out. What happened to him subsequent to that is not my concern."

"This was an attack on my family–on *me*– perpetrated by a faction that resides here, beneath this roof."

"Nobody at this Academy is permitted a family, Acolyte, and that most certainly includes you. I struck your father down because he contravened this law." The Chancellor straightened up, clasped his left fist in his right hand. "If I take action now, I am condoning what I have previously forbidden."

I was still furious, but I understood his quandary. "This was intended to provoke you."

"No," said the Chancellor. "The Faction already knows my position on this. They know I cannot be provoked. But you, Acolyte..."

"I am not bound from action, as you are."

"You must not respond," said the Chancellor. "You are playing into their hands."

"No, Chancellor," I replied. "I will not play anybody else's hand–not even yours."

"That is what they are counting on. That is why you are weak."

"We'll see about that." I turned to leave.

"Acolyte..."

I stopped and looked back at the Chancellor, who was once more seated.

"Acolyte, you show a measure of talent. Your mastery of the Naming Art is impressive for one of your age, and your studies of...other...disciplines have given you many advantages over your peers. But your enemies are many, and you cannot stand against them all."

"I see."

"Students may tussle and scrap amongst themselves. Sometimes their injuries are grave. Sometimes students die. That is the way of the Academy. But I will not permit any acolyte to act against the faculty—no matter the cause. Do you understand me?"

"Chancellor, do you truly doubt my capacity to understand what you are saying?"

The Chancellor pressed his hands together. "No, Acolyte, I do not. The issue is your capacity to obey the rules I have set down."

I shrugged. "In that, Chancellor, we will be forever at odds. I will protect myself from my enemies if you will not. If your reckoning must then be with me, I will deal with you as well."

The Chancellor stood silently for a moment. The last person to threaten him directly had been my father.

"This is a dark path you tread, Acolyte."

Now the Chancellor was starting to sound like Thieu. I swallowed a mouthful of bile and said, "It is your choices that have put me on it."

"I spared your life, Acolyte."

"Yes, Chancellor, you did," I replied. "I expect that seems like a mistake now."

Saad was responsible for the death of my parents. I was certain of it.

Professor Thieu had shown too much concern over my father's fate; too much hope that he could be restored. Saad was less sentimental and more ambitious. The Faction might still find a way to displace the Chancellor, and it would be easier for him to contest Thieu for supremacy when his own time came. Saad had profited from my father's machinations, and now he would profit from his death.

Saad and Arakne had been accepted into the social circle of the students from the cohort senior to our own. So had Boudreaux, although he was now a lesser light. The golden shine had come off him as he grew out of childhood, but he was still a talented player.

Members of the senior cohort were preparing to be elevated to positions within the faculty. It was rumored that Saad might win his robe before any of them. He was powerful and clever beyond his years, he was well liked, and he had influential allies.

If I was going to move against him, it would have to be soon, before his promotion. The Chancellor had practically said as much.

I waited until it was dark.

———◄ ● ►———

The mind is the central mystery of our universe.

We can observe the brain tissue that provides a substrate for the mind. We can observe the flow of blood through this tissue, the electrical impulses that spark across it. We can observe how the body it controls responds to the world around it. But we cannot observe a mind directly.

We cannot observe sentience itself: that intangible construct, generated from base matter and measurable energy, which is aware of itself as a distinct being, which knows itself separate from the world and from other sentients.

Mind is the purview of the artist. To perceive that which one's eyes cannot, to extend one's consciousness and volition beyond the boundaries of one's senses: that is the art of the sorcerer. To travel the fictive places, beyond matter, beyond material reality: that is the life of the magus.

I did not cast a light to guide my way through the hallways of the Academy that night. After my years spent in the Library of Shadows, I did not need one. I was most comfortable in the darkness.

Mind is the habitat of the magician, and it is a perilous one. Consciousness lives in the darkest places, and that landscape is not empty. It is corrugated with shoals and reefs, riven with ditches and trenches. The tides are strange, and their dangers are difficult to perceive, much less comprehend.

To swim beyond your own sensorium, while maintaining full consciousness, is like walking around with your organs on the outside. You are chum in the water. How can you protect yourself from the sharks?

Let us say that you can manage it. Let us say that you can invert your consciousness without destroying it, that you can hold your selves together and navigate the darkness while fending off the predators that harry you. Let us say that you have learned to do this. There is still a difference between survival and hunting.

It was easy to find Saad. His mind was lit up like Times Square on New Year's Eve. The door to his room stood open, and light spilled out through it into the hallway.

I went through it, and my shadow followed at my heels.

I was surprised at the austerity of Saad's room. A shelf, a sleeping palette, a chest. No decorations. No luxuries. Saad's showy exterior concealed a serious and dangerous practitioner.

Saad was sitting on the palette with his legs folded beneath him, his hands resting open on his thighs. His eyes were closed. He was wearing threadbare trousers and a yellowing vest, which I supposed were the clothes in which he had arrived at the Academy. I had come from a sheltered middle-class America; Saad had come from second-world poverty.

"Welcome, Acolyte," he said, in a near-perfect imitation of the Chancellor's sonorous tones. His eyes remained closed. "Have you come seeking the Mystery?"

"There is no mystery," I replied. "I know it was you who killed my parents."

He only smiled at me. "They died in a fire, my friend."

"Which you started."

"That was careless of me."

I just stood there.

He sighed and rolled his eyes. "Have you come to fight me, then?"

"No, Saad. I have come to kill you."

Saad opened his eyes when I spoke his name. He opened his mouth, too, but he could not speak.

He put his hand to his chest, as if to cover some wound—as if he could keep in the magic that was hemorrhaging from it. But he could not. He had not prepared himself for this. He had not believed it could happen. He had not believed that I would know his name.

I took another step into the room. Saad stared up at me, his mouth working, but all he could issue was a choking sound. Whatever he had left to say, I did not care to hear it. I certainly had no speech prepared for him.

"Die," I said.

He did as I instructed.

Act 8.

— MEAT AND CONSEQUENCES
—

What does it mean to kill a man? I meditated long upon the question. I wanted to see if the experience had changed me.

What does it mean to kill a man? To still his motion; to disperse his energy; to consign his body to rot; to collapse the waveform of his consciousness; to scatter his mind into a cascade of electrons?

It means exactly that and nothing more.

With discipline it is possible to transcend the bio-electrical life into which we are born. Brain tissue is not the only substrate capable of hosting a mind. Consciousness can migrate from one medium to another, if it is properly prepared. If it is invested with the Art, and the will. I myself am proof of that.

But I do not believe in the soul. I do not believe there is some indestructible portion of the self that will persist through the eons of this universe, or will eventually transition into worlds more profound than this one. All worlds are equally profound.

I do not believe in heaven and hell. I do not believe in good and evil, though most would surely judge me in the latter category.

I felt nothing for Saad's death. No sorrow, no remorse, no pride, no satisfaction. Saad had claimed to be my friend, but he had acted as my enemy. I suppose that he was both. But whatever he had been to me, Saad was, above all else, a threat.

Saad was a truer son to my father than I was. My father had given him everything he had denied me— and Saad had killed him when it became expedient. I expect that my father would have encouraged such ruthlessness.

I was jealous, though it was not jealousy that drove me to murder. I wanted vengeance, but I did not kill Saad for revenge. I killed him because he opposed me.

Now that he was gone, so was that jealousy and, with it, the desire for vengeance. There would be consequences for my actions, of course, but I had dealt with the immediate threat.

That is all that remains of a person when they are gone: meat and consequences.

It was hunger that finally drove me from my meditations. There was nothing left to introspect, and there was nothing left in my belly. I put the matter from my mind and left my room in search of sustenance.

As I wound my way to the Refectory the corridors were empty, but I barely noticed. I was scarcely cognizant of the time of day. I was just hungry, and that was the only real thought in my head as I pushed through the doors into the dining hall.

I had never seen the place filled to capacity before. I had never seen so many of the faculty and students together in one room. I don't know if it was the entire population of the school, but it felt as if everybody I knew was present, and many more besides. Everybody I had seen walking the halls or skulking in the classrooms. Everybody was there, but for the Chancellor. Nobody was eating.

I stopped just inside the threshold. It seemed that my dinner would to have to wait.

I thought about turning and fleeing. I did not care if they thought me a coward, but I knew that there was no possibility of escape. I stood my ground.

There was a churning motion at the center of the crowd. Then it parted and Thieu came forward. The hubbub subsided.

He stood for a moment before he spoke. "Acolyte, you have some explaining to do."

"I am not accountable to you."

"I am the Professor of Art. All students are accountable to me, if I demand it."

"You saying it does not make it true, Professor."

I knew that fear was feeding his anger–but now I realized that he didn't fear my abilities. He was indeed the Professor of Art; I was just a student.

Thieu feared me because, for all his own power, he could not intimidate me.

"You killed another student."

I shrugged. "Students die. The Chancellor himself told me that."

Arakne, standing near to a door on the far side of the room, fixed me with unblinking black eyes. I met her gaze calmly.

"He acted in self-defense." The voice was not one I had ever expected to hear speaking for me. "The dead boy was a threat to him."

"A threat?" Thieu's tone was incredulous.

"The dead boy killed his father," said Boudreaux. "He was only trying to protect himself."

"His father!" replied Thieu. The words were shrill in the sudden silence.

Arakne stood, upsetting a chair behind her. Everybody turned to stare. She was breathing hard. With a grunt, she turned and stalked out of the room. Though she held herself well, I could see her hands shaking. I could not guess if it was from rage or sorrow. In hindsight, it may have been simple fear.

Boudreaux cleared his throat.

"His father," said Thieu. "No family is permitted to those who join the Academy. You know this as well as I do, Acolyte."

Boudreaux shrugged. "We all have fathers, Professor. None of us have any say in the matter."

"Now we have come to the bones of the matter," said Maruyama. I had not seen her push her way through the crowd, but now she was at the front of it, standing only meters from the professor.

"The boy's father was cast out from the Academy for the crime of siring this...abomination...who stands before us," said Thieu. "But this one's crimes are worse than any of his father's misadventures. He has brought a grievance from outside of the Academy into these halls. Now my most promising student lies dead, at his hand."

I wanted to interject that I had not employed either of my hands in the deed, but Maruyama got in first. Foolish though I was, I was not foolish enough to interrupt someone who was speaking in my defense.

"That is rich coming from you, Professor," she replied. "If the matter has propagated beyond the walls of the Academy, it is as much your fault as anybody's."

"What are you implying?"

"You were conspiring with the boy's father long before he showed up on our doorstep. We all know it. You worshipped the man—I cannot fathom your problem with his child."

"This *child*..."

"I am no child," I replied. I was eighteen.

"You are a depthless imitation of a great man," replied Thieu. "A murdering abomination with no right to the life you have inherited."

"That inheritance has come at a substantial cost to the boy," replied Maruyama. "I find it difficult to begrudge him of it."

"He killed another student."

"This is a difficult place to live. Students die here all the time, Professor, and usually with far less cause."

"They do indeed." Thieu raised a hand toward me and clenched his fingers. The power he drew was immense, and the force he exerted upon me drove me to my knees. The pressure compressed my ribs, squirting the breath from my lungs and holding them closed. Gasping, I raised my own hands and tried to find a trance, tried to slip into a state from which I could draw upon my own power.

I glimpsed other energies taking shape—Maruyama rallying to my defense—but before she could, a new presence fell upon the room, extinguishing every working like a fire-blanket.

"That will be enough." The Chancellor's voice was just loud enough that I could hear it over the ringing in my ears.

Thieu's attack lost coherence, and the pressure on my chest abated. I put my head in between my knees and choked in some oxygen. A paroxysm of coughing followed.

"Enough," said the Chancellor again. He spoke quietly, but his words were large enough to fill the silence. "Enough. One student's death will suffice for today. Be gone, all of you."

The Refectory emptied out while I recovered myself. By the time I was back on my feet, only the Chancellor remained.

"Did you think that wise?" he said. "To face down the entire Academy, alone?"

"It wasn't the entire school," I replied. "*You* weren't present."

"You think I will come and save you the next time such foolishness comes over you?"

"I just wanted some dinner," I replied. "But no, Chancellor, I do not. Next time, you will have to save them from me."

Arakne was waiting for me in my empty room. She had braced herself, like a spider, in a cornice at the back of the room, using both arms and legs. I am not easily intimidated, but the sight of her up there, staring down at me with those reflector eyes, stopped me in my tracks.

Arakne had smashed all of my newest wards and I hadn't felt a thing. She looked alien and dangerous, every inch the beast she was named for. I had faced down the Chancellor, and Professor Thieu, and my own father, but none of them had provoked such a visceral pang of fear in me.

"I like what you've done with the place," said Arakne. Her voice was like silk: smooth and soft and unbreakably strong.

"Hello."

I still hadn't eaten. When the Chancellor had escorted me out of the Refectory, it had seemed inappropriate to ask if I could grab some take-out. My stomach rumbled.

"So it's true," said Arakne. "You killed him."

I clenched my jaw and shook off the horror. "Of course I killed him."

"I thought it would go the other way. How did you do it?"

"I spoke his name and then I instructed him to die."

Arakne's eight eyes glittered as she moved her head. I could not understand what the gesture was supposed to indicate. "What was his name?"

"Saad."

Her head tilted left. "How did you find out?"

"I wouldn't tell you, even if I knew."

Arakne looked down, so that only her topmost eyes were visible. "You really don't know, do you? You don't know anything."

"I know he killed my family."

"And so you killed him. You killed Saad."

"I'm not going to pretend I'm sorry."

"I didn't expect that you would."

We faced each other in silence for a moment. "What do you want from me?" I asked.

"What do I want from you? From *you*?"

An unexpected and irrational hope arose that she wanted sex. I dismissed it quickly. It was just biology, like the hunger in my guts.

Arakne's mouth twisted around her mandibles. "You think I'm his...you think I was just Saad's little girlfriend, don't you? His devoted follower. His arm candy."

I said nothing.

"I spent years with him. With them. The Faction. Listening to all their talk, their speculation, their plans. Mostly listening to them go on about your father–and about you."

"Should I be flattered?"

"They wondered what secrets you kept. What depths you concealed. But there's nothing, is there? You're just an empty reflection. You are a shadow cast by a cardboard cut-out."

"I am my father's son. I cannot change that."

Arakne shook her head. There were strands of web growing through her hair. Tiny spiders crawled all through it. I suppressed a shudder. It was all the more horrifying for the fact that I found it arousing.

"You really don't know anything," she said. "You don't even *suspect* the truth."

"You're against them," I said. "Against the Faction. Against my father, and Saad, and the Professor of Art, and whoever else is behind this lunacy. You're a spy for the Chancellor."

"Well, would you look at that?" said Arakne. "Just when I had given up hope, the Miracle Boy finds a single clue."

"You were on my side."

"I have been trying to protect you since the day you arrived here," she said.

"When I came back from the Library of Shadows..."

"The spider charm, yes. It was a ward of protection."

"I thought that was a practical joke. A 'kick me.'"

"Saad was supposed to think that. *You* were supposed to know better."

"How was I to know that?"

Arakne fixed me with those eyes of hers. Her mandibles worked.

"You know you're dead, don't you? The Chancellor saved you this time, but he has levelled no rebuke against the Professor of Art. He will come for you again, sooner or later, and next time he will make sure there is nobody there to stop him."

"I'll be ready for him."

"No. No, you won't. He has decades of experience on you. He has power and knowledge and art and wisdom. And you? You have a handful of shadow tricks and a dead father that he once feared and worshipped. Next time the professor finds you alone he will kill you. I don't think he will wait very long."

"And what about you?"

"I'm done. I'm out of here. The Faction is undergoing a...restructuring...in the wake of its recently depleted numbers. It's only a matter of time before they figure out my part in all of this."

"You want me to go with you."

Arakne's mandibles clacked together when she laughed. "No. No, I don't want you anywhere near to me. You have a target on you–a big, red bulls-eye. The professor will find you wherever you go. You've cost him too much. And the Chancellor cannot afford to help you again."

"Will the Chancellor fall?"

"I don't think so. The Faction is weak now. Your father is gone, Saad is gone, and you are lost to them. They will have their retribution on you, but they know better than to challenge the Chancellor in the present circumstances. They will sort out their own internal divisions and seek to rebuild, now."

"You're telling me to flee."

"Far be it from me to tell the great Scion of Darkness what to do," said Arakne. "I'm telling you goodbye. Do whatever you like."

She strode from the room and shut the door behind her. Were there spider webs hanging in the darkened corners? Nests of tiny spiders? I wanted to cleanse the room with fire. I wanted to see something burn.

Arakne was right. I wouldn't survive another confrontation with the professor. Thieu's attack had demonstrated to everyone what I truly was: a shadow cast large by a trick of perspective. I was powerless to harm those with true dimension. And yet...

And yet I had killed Saad, the Faction's favored son. I had defeated my own father, inside his own psyche. I was smart. I was ruthless. I was dangerous, because I did not respect the rules. But even in my hubris, I knew that I was outmatched.

What could change the equation in my favor? Perhaps the Chancellor's book. The Book of Names. If I could steal it; if I could decode it...

I abandoned the idea as quickly as it occurred to me. It felt like a trap. If I could get away with it, I would turn the Chancellor against me. Besides, I already knew the names of my enemies. What would I truly gain from it?

Arakne was right. I needed to flee. But I was only a student. Since the Chancellor had sealed my father's Way back to New York, I had no way to travel from the Academy, and I did not think I would get very far if I set out on foot.

I could think of only one sanctuary. There was only one place that I could go where nobody would dare to follow.

I would return to the Library of Shadows.

Act 9.

— WALKING SHADOW —

I thought I would leave the sensation of hunger behind when I returned to the Library of Shadows, but through all the time I spent among the stacks something ravenous howled at the core of me, demanding fuel–and the only fuel available was information. I think it was my hunger that drew the attention of the other Readers.

The first time I sojourned in the Library, they paid me little heed. I was young and earnest and I had a genuine need for the knowledge I sought. This time was different. This time I was even more voracious, and the Readers saw in me a kindred spirit–or, at least, a kindred shadow.

You could say they took me under their wings–or flukes, or cloaks. The Readers in the Library of Shadows are metaphysical beings, as much metaphor as fact. There are no players among them, no characters strutting the boards for an audience that may or may not exist. They are dark things, living in the darkest places; existing more truly in the works they read than they do in any material reality.

The Readers taught me by example. I watched them school and swarm around the most feculent works; I watched them devour the ripest and sweetest tomes; I watched them hunt down the rarest fruits in the most obscure of books and ravish them. I watched them, and I did as they did.

Like a ray, I would skate over the pages, sucking up quantities of raw learning. I spread myself wide to ride the currents of knowledge up to the highest strata; I unrolled my being to harvest the tiniest protozoans of truth.

But the Library of Shadows was not some undersea idyll. There was competition for the more esoteric victuals. The deeper into the stacks one ventured, the deeper ran the feuds and factions. Some days there were pitched battles; other days offered guerrilla skirmishes.

I learned to fight in the Library, and while the combat itself was abstract and the blood spilled was mostly ink, the threat of death was real enough. But the fighting was worth it, for the prizes we sought were the most valuable things of all: knowledge and power.

I studied the Arts, of course. I plied the Mysteries. The Naming Art of the Academy was a vast topic in its own right, but I soon found detours into the runes and lines of the graphomancers; the directional cants of the topomancers; the flames and furnaces of the pyromancers; the bones and stones of the geomancers.

I sampled the sympathetic magic of the shamans, too—for I had known one, briefly, and she had been good to me—but I found no affinity for that art.

I studied everything that drew my attention, but I was no dilettante. I studied hard and long and, while I may not have achieved mastery of those other forms, I learned enough to count myself expert.

And there were darker arts. Arts that dealt in the currency of death and nightmares and horror. Demons, destruction, annihilation, abnegation, apocalypse. The Readers who sought these arts were hideous, shapeless, unfathomable things--but they did not frighten me. Who would go to a place called the Library of Shadows and be surprised to find darkness there? Who would go to the Biblioteca Tenebrae unless they were invested with a darkness of their own?

I had lost all concept of time. I had gone native among the stacks. I still knew my name, but I came to regard the being denoted by it as somebody separate from my shadow-self. Quay was an earlier form, wrapped now in a cocoon of darkness. The longer I remained there, the less coherent that form became. Eventually it would be consumed entirely as I became something...other.

Still, I recognized the Librarian. It was a chromatic black, where this world was only gray shadow. It was sharply angled, where the interior of the Library was blurred and indistinct. It was an ordering force imposed upon a system that tended to disorder.

~Quay.

I could not communicate with any of the Readers the way I communicated with the Librarian. It had some meta-level access to my intellect that was opaque to the other residents of the Library. I think it understood me better than any of the beings with whom I had once shared my material existence. But I was not so foolish as to mistake this understanding as some concern about my welfare.

~Yes, Librarian?

~One of your kind has been asking after you.

Now it really had my attention.

~Is he still here?

~No. He was here only briefly.

~What did he want?

~To know if you were here.

~Did you tell him?

~I did not say anything. I am a librarian, not a warden.

~Who was it?

~I will not tell you his name.

Of course it would not. It had refused my father the same request.

~And yet he knows mine.

~Of course. How else could he ask after you?

~Why have you brought me this information, Librarian?

~The one who seeks you is not welcome here. I do not wish him to return.

~I thought all were welcome in the Library?

~Those that come here to study are welcome. Those who come to spy on the habits of others are not. This is a place of learning–I will not have politics disrupt it.

~And me, Librarian? Are you asking me to leave?

~You are a Reader. You have as much right to be here as any other. The place you have left behind is your concern, not mine.

The Librarian twisted out of my presence, and I stood there alone, but with much to ponder about the life I had almost forgotten.

Who had sought me here? Thieu seemed the most likely candidate. Arakne had warned that he would come for me. That his courage had failed when the Librarian refused to hand me over did not surprise me. The question was, what would I do about it?

I could have stayed in the Library. I could have remained a Reader forever. I could have let my being dwindle until I was but a wisp of shadow, content to live in that half-world of unrecorded learning and abstract thought. I could have drifted there until my self discorporated entirely. It would have been a pleasant way to go, but I now found myself unwilling to relinquish the material existence I had found so uncomfortable.

I did not like the thought of Thieu coming here, even if it was only to peer across the threshold, hoping to see what I was doing. Some pride remained to me yet. If I remained here, victory was his. I could not allow such a weak, old fool to better me.

If I had remained there among the stacks, would I have become something less monstrous than the thing I have become? I cannot say.

This much I know for certain: anything that does what I have done is a monster, whether it walks as a man or not.

Although my second sojourn in the Library lasted longer than the first, the return to my own body was less of an ordeal the second time.

Six years had elapsed. I was an adult now. My bones had hardened, but I had not grown appreciably. Even so, I felt stronger, more confident. I did not have to bear up under a constant wash of hormones and chemical changes to keep my identity in focus.

And I was still ravenously hungry.

I went first to the Refectory. It was mid-morning, and there were few people around. Nobody took notice of me as I made my way through the halls, though I did nothing to conceal myself.

Perhaps I walked in shadow, but I would not have called this a working. It was a habit learned in a place of silence and darkness. It was a simple desire not to be disturbed; it was not any sorcery or spell that I set with will.

The Refectory served the same noodles and broth it always did. I took three portions and consumed them plain. I took no pleasure in it, but it drove the

hunger pains from my belly. And yet I still felt unsa-
tisfied. I was still hungry, but not for food.

I went next to the showers. The pounding water
and the clouds of steam drew about me like some
ethereal world, where air and water held sway over
the other elements. I felt my alignment with the void
shift, finally, and when I stepped out of the water,
the earth was reassuringly solid beneath my feet.
Fires guttered and flared inside me, and my blood
felt hot in my veins.

It was not my habit to look at myself. Introspection
and meditation are the ways of the magician; the
surface flesh is of little consequence. But I passed a
mirror as I left the showers, and I did not turn my
eyes away. The reflection I beheld stopped me in my
tracks.

I saw my father in the glass. A leaner, younger
version than I had ever met, perhaps, but I recognized him well enough. The same beardless face,
the same long, dark hair, the same black eyes. But
there was something lacking in this version of him.
Some quality was missing.

My father was dark, while I merely stood in
his shadow. My father had surety, but all I had
was hubris. My father had presence; I was but an
apparition.

Suddenly furious, I drew a curtain across the
mirror's surface. It would never again show me
truths I did not wish to see. I left the mirror
blackened, so that any who wished to see their

reflections in its glass must peer down into the shadows.

I felt no need to visit my room. It had been empty when I had fled to the Library of Shadows, and I doubted that had changed in the years I had been gone. Or perhaps Arakne's spiders had overrun it. Six years had passed–perhaps some new student had taken possession of it. I didn't care. There was nothing in there I needed.

I was back at school. Perhaps it was time I went back to class.

It took me a moment to recognize him in his robe, but I was not really surprised to discover that Boudreaux was now teaching the acolytes. He had won his place on the faculty while I was gone.

Boudreaux spoke to the class more cogently than Professor Thieu, but with less authority. He seemed smaller in the robe, though he had grown while I was away. He was taller than I was, now, and he carried more bulk.

The class, too, seemed smaller than before. Less populous. There were new students–a fresh intake– as well as a handful of holdovers from my own cohort, but numbers were certainly down. Saad was dead. Arakne was gone. I could find no names for any of the new students.

My appearance charged the room with an energy I don't think it had seen in many years. Boudreaux's teeth clicked audibly as he bit off his monologue.

Those students who recognized me looked shocked; those who did not, only puzzled.

I stood facing Boudreaux for moments before either of us spoke. "Congratulations," I said. "Are you now the Professor of Art?"

Boudreaux shook his head. "I do not claim that title. You may call me Doctor," he said. He spoke formally now, like the rest of the faculty, and had moderated his accent. He seemed embarrassed.

"Doctor. Very good," I replied. "That will make my next query less confusing. Where is the professor?"

Boudreaux's gaze flickered to the doorway, and then back to me. "I don't think you will have too much difficulty finding him," he said.

Despite our bad blood, Boudreaux had supported me when Thieu had called for my death. I did not think he would stand with me against my enemy, but I was grateful for the warning.

I turned with the class toward the figure that came bustling through the doorway.

Professor Thieu was obviously angry. Angry that I had eluded him before, angry that I had returned, and, I expect, angry that I looked so much like my father.

"From which hole have you just crawled, Acolyte?"

Students scurried away as he strode into the room, leaving a clear space between us.

"The deepest one there is," I replied.

"Soon you will occupy another. I fear it will be somewhat shallower."

"We all go to the grave, Professor," I replied. "Though some fear it more than others."

Thieu came toward me. "Whether you are fearless or merely glib, Acolyte, I have no patience for it. Your time here is over."

I felt him drawing the energies he had used to crush me during our earlier confrontation in the Refectory. This time I was ready for it.

"Why is it, then, that you sought me in the Library, Professor?" I asked.

Thieu snorted. "Acolyte, I would no more have sought you in the Library than I would a cockroach in the sewers of Paris."

"Well, somebody did," I replied, "and I cannot think who it might have been besides you, Professor Thieu."

He faltered when I spoke his name. I saw his focus slip, the energies spill from between his splayed fingers. But it was not like it had been with Saad. He felt the blow, but it was not a fatal strike.

Thieu smiled. "Ah. That was your secret, eh, boy? That was the source of your arrogance. You have learned some names."

Thieu found his center and began to draw power again. He had shrugged off my best attack as if it were nothing.

"We all know *your* name, of course, but nobody has dared to speak it. Now you have spoken mine, and it was not the weapon you had hoped."

I stepped behind a pillar. The shadows were soft there, but they were deep enough for my purposes. I inhaled the darkness and set my own focus.

While this was a different sort of conflict to that waged in the Library of Shadows, I was by now well-conditioned to the danger of combat. My chief weapon had failed me; now I must resort to tactics and guile. I had wanted to make a quick killing, but instead I was going to have to fight.

Thieu made a slicing motion with his hand. Stone sprayed horizontally as my protective pillar split apart. I threw myself away from it, naming a hasty shield to protect me from falling masonry. The professor could have ruptured me just as easily as he had destroyed the column. I would not let him have that opportunity again.

I was near the window, and the sunlight stung my eyes. I turned my face away, set my eyes upon my streaming shadow. In the Library, I would have used it to conceal myself. Was this place so different?

Boudreaux raised a shield to protect himself and the students. I did not hear him speak the working. He had learned his lesson, and he had clearly earned his place on the faculty. "Move!" he yelled. "All of you. Move. Now!"

Most of the students did as instructed, although some hung back to see what would happen next. I felt no concern for their safety.

I drew the darkness around me as a cloak and started to work my way around the perimeter of the room. It was difficult to turn invisible in this manner, but I hoped it would render me *dim* to the eyes of my enemy.

Thieu stood his ground. "I am *faculty*, Acolyte. Do you understand what that means?" He spoke in the same drone he used to deliver his lectures, trying to lull me while he searched the room. "It means that I have begun my ascension to the Mystery. The name I once wore means less and less to me all the time."

A pause. He had found me. I could practically hear the smile on his lips. "If there is one thing I have learned from your father's plight, it is this: let go of your name. It will only weigh you down in your rise to power."

A succession of columns erupted behind me as I sprinted down the hall. I was unused to the material world, and it was taking me longer than I had thought to raise proper defenses. The shadows were thinner here, and more easily disrupted.

I had thought myself prepared for this, but I had seen my father resist when the Chancellor had named him; I should have expected that Thieu would be similarly resilient.

"Do you hear me, Acolyte? A true magician will *rise* to power. You, on the other hand, have sought your learning in the gutter."

Thieu made a gesture, and the ceiling along the eastern wall of the classroom fell as the columns supporting it collapsed. I dove for a gap in the wall, and another blast clipped me, pushing me through it sideways.

Suddenly I was outside of the Academy, arms flailing, legs kicking. I was flying. The wind caught my hair, flapped my garments. The clouds spread golden below me, and the sun, above, was near to its meridian. The air was thin, and I could barely breathe, no matter how hard I inhaled.

The stepped marble walls of the Academy rotated through my field of vision as I tumbled away from it. My shadow was the only blemish on its austere, white surface.

My shadow. I quelled the panic and called to the darkness. Black tendrils peeled from the Academy walls, stretched out to me. They touched the soles of my shoes and reconnected.

I shut my eyes and commanded my shadow to reel me in. I felt a tugging on my feet and then a sudden change in direction, as though I had reached the furthest extent of an elastic cord and now it was snapping me back in the direction from which I had come. I stopped thrashing with my arms and legs and braced myself as I came out of the spin.

My feet struck the wall of the Academy with enough force to send stinging shocks up both of my legs. Now I was stationary, although I could feel gravity tugging me in a direction I no longer understood to be "down."

I was dizzy. Hyperventilating. I inhaled slowly and deeply, sucking in oxygen-rich air from the Academy's artificial climate. I exhaled to flush the panic from my system and opened my eyes.

Blue sky. I looked toward my feet and saw that they were adhering to one of the Academy's walls with my shadow puddled around them.

I took an experimental step. Darkness clung to the sole of my shoe like tar. Another step, turning. Another. Now I was facing downward.

The hole that Thieu had smashed through the side of the building was a good twenty meters above me. I set out for it, shakily at first, but quickly learning to trust in the adhesive power of my shadow. My legs burned with the effort of keeping myself perpendicular to the wall.

The Chancellor would be here soon. I had only a short time to end this.

Thieu leaned out of the gap in the wall, peering down to see where I had fallen. I threw a line of shadow toward him. It tore through the ragged air and gouged a ruler-straight scar into the side of the building.

The professor batted it away with a contemptuous wave of his hand. He looked down at me, craning his neck, and said, "Thank you for that, Acolyte. Now nobody can accuse me of slaying a defenseless student."

I looked up at him from my vantage, stuck to the side of the building like a gnat taking rest. I had no reply.

"I cannot say I have ever enjoyed your company," said Thieu, "but I am certain I will enjoy your death. For that, if nothing else, I thank you, Mr. Qua–"

I reached into the professor's throat and named his airways closed before he could finish saying my name.

"Professor Thieu," I said, "I know you are supposed to be a teacher, but I always thought you talked too much."

His eyes rolled toward me, and his hands went to his throat. I had the advantage now, but my shadow tricks would not hold up in a contest of direct power.

I remembered Sensei Maruyama's first lesson: a small amount of power, carefully applied, is far more effective than a massive exertion poorly planned.

I reached into his chest and pinched off the supply of blood to his heart. The professor's face went from red to purple to black. He pitched forward and lay still, hanging halfway out of the building.

I walked up the side of the building and allowed my shadow to lift me into the classroom through the gap in the wall. I had to kick past Thieu's corpse in order to get through, but for once he was not concerned with my insolence.

If any students had remained to witness the end of the fight, they had now fled. Rubble had blocked most of the windows, which were on the eastern side of the room, but light spilled in through the collapsed roof. The sky was visible through the hole, bright and clear and beautiful. I stood there a while, taking in the extent of the damage, enjoying the sunlight on my skin and the cooling breeze.

When I turned back to the shadows, I found them more welcoming than ever.

Act 10.

— IN THE FADE —

The window behind the Chancellor's desk showed a wall of solid black too dark to be the night sky. The room was lit by dozens of candles, but none of them cast any reflection upon the glass. Perhaps there was no glass at all. Perhaps the Chancellor sat with his back to the open void.

The Chancellor looked older than ever—and more powerful. His enemies had been vanquished and, now, he had but one last problem to address.

"Thank you for coming, Acolyte." The Chancellor had the great tome open in front of him. I glanced at it, but I still could not read anything written on its pages.

"I do not believe you have summoned me here to receive your gratitude."

He sighed. "You have the right of it, of course."

The Chancellor closed his book. He turned over the cover with one hand, with no visible effort. He was stronger than he looked—or perhaps the book was less substantial than it appeared.

"Let's get on with it, then."

"Acolyte, I have been far too lenient with you in the past. If you cannot abide by our rules, I cannot allow you to study here."

I knew it then. The book of names—and all of the tomes on the shelves behind him—were props. Fakes. Traps for desperate young acolytes looking for an easy route to power. That was why I couldn't read them.

The window, also, was fake. The Chancellor himself was the only thing in the room that was authentic.

"It was you who came to find me in the Library of Shadows," I said. "You knew it would draw me back here. You knew this would be the outcome."

The Chancellor adjusted his spectacles and said, "That is true, but it does not change the situation. You made your own choices, just as your father did before you."

"Why is it that this always comes back to my father?" The words were like bile on my tongue.

"There is a reason we do not permit families here, and I fear that you have conclusively proven the need for the stricture to remain. Blood will out, Mr. Quay. Dynasties cast long shadows."

A name is a nail that pins us to the world. I had thought that my initial failure to strike at Thieu was due to a lack of force behind the blow, but the Chancellor showed me otherwise. It is the angle of the blow that drives the nail straight as much as the weight of the hammer.

I was prepared for it. I had watched Saad die from such a wound, and I had practiced ways to mitigate the damage. I could not shrug off the blow the same way Thieu had shrugged off mine–the Chancellor was far too deft–but at least I could staunch the bleeding.

I plugged the hole with shadow and did my best to prevent my power from spilling out all at once. Perhaps I could keep some dregs of it if I sealed the wound quickly. Perhaps I could retain enough for some final working.

I crossed my arms and held my chin high. It was all I could do to remain upright.

The Chancellor was unimpressed by my fortitude. "Do you have anything more to say?"

I could not have spoken if I wanted to.

"Then I bid you leave the Academy, and do not return," said the Chancellor. "The Mysteries will never be yours."

———◖●◗———

I staggered out into the snow of the mountain passes, lost and freezing, disoriented and weak from my injuries.

The Chancellor had given me a coat, but it did little to cut the gusting wind. Flurries of snow clouded my vision.

I had no idea where I was–which country, what latitude, what planet–but I did know the direction I was headed. I was going down.

If the Chancellor hadn't sealed my father's Way back to Manhattan, perhaps I could have used it, but he was not going to open it again for the likes of me. I had my pride and my rage, but neither of those was enough to keep me from freezing to death. Even my shadow had deserted me in the blinding white.

I went down into bright oblivion, and I thought it was my end.

Act II.

THROUGH A
— GLASS DARKLY —

I awoke to the smell of sweat and boiled cabbage. There was something strangely soft and textured beneath me. It took minutes for me to figure out what it was: a rumpled sheet on a mattress.

When I opened my eyes, I found myself staring across an expanse of tattered pink blanket at a mildewed wall.

I was lying on an unsupported mattress in a small, windowless room. The only other furnishings were a single chair, a wardrobe, and a dresser, which was covered with books and bottles of makeup. The mirror standing over it was cracked. The room was only just large enough to accommodate all of these items.

It was twice as large as my cell at the Academy.

I stood up and found I was naked. The Chancellor's coat lay draped on the solitary chair, and my ancient tennis shoes lay beneath it. I couldn't see the rest of my clothes.

When Hana opened the door, I was not in the least bit surprised.

"Good morning, Quay," she said, and she smiled like she meant it.

I flinched, hearing my name, but the spike was already in me and the agony of it quickly subsided to a dull ache. "Hana."

"Welcome to London," she said. She was holding a pile of freshly laundered clothing.

"I thought..." It took a moment for me to gather the information. I was not operating at full capacity. "I thought you were going to New York."

Hana shrugged. "Easier to get a work visa here."

"I've never been to London before."

It was a foolish thing to say. I'd never been anywhere, and she knew it as well as I did. "Well, you're here now," she replied. "You'll like it."

I didn't even blink. "I don't think so."

Hana thought about it for a moment. "Well, maybe you won't," she said, "but you *will* have fun."

I doubted that too.

"Come on," she said, throwing the pile of clothing onto the bed. "Let's get some breakfast in you."

We left the house, which was a narrow, two-story place in the suburb Hana told me was called Wimbledon. "You know, where they play tennis."

"I don't know anything about tennis."

Apparently, she shared the place with half a dozen other foreigners. Hana said the rent was cheap, for London. I had no idea what rent was supposed to cost. I'd never had a job. I'd never lived anywhere but my parents' home and the Academy.

Although Hana told me it was summer, the skies were gray and I was shivering in my t-shirt and jeans. The smell of laundry detergent was strange and foreign to me. I felt weak and mildly nauseated.

I'd lost muscle mass and my gait was stiff and slow. I didn't know how long my legs would support my weight. I'd been thin to begin with, but now I was close to emaciated. My waistband was loose, and my jeans flapped around my shins.

We went into a café in a row of shops up on the main road near a Tube station. It wasn't like Brooklyn, which was dirty and brown and decaying from the inside out. Here the buildings were gray and old on the outside, but inside everything was clean and new.

I slumped, panting, into my chair. When the waitress came, I was still out of breath, so Hana ordered for both of us.

While we waited for our meals to arrive, Hana regarded me with a pity so evident that even I could recognize it. The look on her face moved something terrible in me.

She shook it off and smiled. "Is this the first time you've been out of the Academy since New York?"

"No," I said. Then, "Yes, I suppose. Bodily, I mean."

Hana nodded slowly. "I heard you spent some more time in the Library of Shadows?"

The old me would have demanded to know where she had heard this. The new me just nodded.

"What was it...what was it like in there?"

"It's hard to describe," I said, feeling ever more foolish. "Dark."

The waitress returned, bearing food. Lots of food. Far more food than I was accustomed to eating.

I couldn't remember the last time I had enjoyed a meal. I had long since ceased to care that the food at the Academy was bland and unvaried. Food was fuel, not a source of pleasure. During my expedition to Manhattan with Saad and Arakne and Hana, all those years ago, I had been too concerned with the conversation to enjoy the pizza. I could barely remember my mother's cooking.

Now, though my appetite was poor, the food laid before me was a wonder. Eggs, toast, fried vegetables, juice, coffee. A feast. My appetite improved, and I ate everything on my plate.

"Hungry, are we?" Hana laughed and passed her own half-finished meal over to me. "Here, why don't you finish mine?"

I did. In the street outside the café, I fell to my knees and vomited everything into the gutter. My stomach was not used to the rich food of the real world.

Over the following weeks, I recovered my health in Hana's care. I met the others with whom we shared a house: Australians, New Zealanders, South Africans, Pakistanis. If any of them were disgruntled that I had joined their situation uninvited, none of them were impolite enough to say so. I never learned to smile at them, but, after some encouragement, I did learn to greet them in the common areas.

I put on enough weight that I no longer resembled a head on a pike. The resemblance to my father returned with my health. Hana told me I should cut my hair, if I really wanted to change my appearance, but I refused. I had lost enough already.

She took me shopping for some new clothes, but despite her best efforts my wardrobe remained a collection of jeans and plain black t-shirts. I did find some boots that were to my liking. My sneakers were not suitable for the soggy English weather. Hana mended the Chancellor's old coat for me, and that was all the clothing I required.

Hana did not have a permanent job, but she always had just enough money for whatever she needed. Rent, groceries, bicycle repairs, Tube tickets. Whenever she needed funds, some friend paid back a loan, or some small job came up, or someone would pay her for a consignment of handmade jewelry that she had left at their store.

Hana cared for sick people. She counseled those in distress. Sometimes, patrons came to her seeking charms or blessings or curses–never under those names, never with such obvious mystical intent–but

Hana always delivered. These people paid her however they could: in barter, in cash, in food, in contraband.

Hana always possessed just enough of everything she needed, even when she needed to share.

It took months before I found the spirit to question her. I was sick all the time. I had lost everything I had worked for. I was finding it difficult to care, difficult to even be curious. I was surprised when the question escaped me, though I knew it needed to be asked.

"Hana," I said.

"Yes, Quay?"

"When I was...expelled from the Academy. Wandering on the slopes. Freezing to death. How did you find me?"

We were drinking tea from a pair of chipped enamel mugs in the back of a rummage store. Hana took a sip from her cup. The tea was still scalding hot from the urn–she sucked on her lips to cool them.

"The Chancellor set you on a Way," she told me. "It led down from the Academy and back into this world. When you crossed over, I knew it."

"How did you know it, Hana?"

She smiled coyly. "We forged a connection when I visited the Academy, Quay. Surely you remember."

I felt my blood in my cheeks. I could not recall the last time I had felt embarrassed, and that only made it all the worse. She laughed, and I could only look away.

Even now I was not certain that she was telling the truth. Hana's magic was subtler than the Naming Art in which I had steeped my life. Often I did not recognize it, unless she identified it to me. Other times it was not magic at all.

"Perhaps the *why* is a more interesting question," she suggested. She blew on her tea and took another sip.

"Why did you save me?"

"Because I like you," she said.

"I am not...likable." I replied, stating the obvious.

Hana looked away. "Everybody loves a bad boy," she replied. Then, "I don't know."

"You felt sorry for me," I said.

Hana smiled. "A little of that, sure."

The old me would have been furious, but the new me did not know how to feel. The new me did not know how to feel about anything. Anger and fear were the only two emotions I knew well enough to recognize.

Hana was powerful, as well as subtle. She would not explain how she had drawn me here from the mountains, but I thought that such a feat was beyond her capabilities. Had her Mistress intervened, then, or some other interested party? Who, and why?

If I was worth saving to some people, I was worth killing to others.

I had no way of knowing who was watching me, and no way to protect myself if the necessity arose. Since the Chancellor had restored my name, I could no longer invoke the Naming Art. If I tried, the smear of power I had saved would be quickly spent, and then I would have no resources left at all.

I resolved to be vigilant. There was little else I could do.

Once I had recovered my health, I quickly grew bored. In the Academy, I burned through my days meditating, practicing, and studying, but there seemed little point in maintaining such discipline now that my Arts were lost to me. I paced the house. I walked through the neighborhood. I rode the Tube.

I had nothing: no money, no papers, no job, nothing. I was nothing in this world—just a blot in the darkest corner of a city full of strangers.

It took time before I would allow Hana to take me out seeking entertainment. I had forgotten the desire to travel that had taken me to the Academy in the first place. I did not know how to act in public, and I was afraid to learn, but boredom eventually got the better of my fear.

Hana took me to the cinema. To rock concerts. To the theater. Windsor Castle, the Houses of Parliament, Westminster Abbey, the Tate and Tate Modern. The Tower of London. Stonehenge and Salisbury. I enjoyed each excursion more than the last.

I was young, unemployed, and foreign. I had time on my hands, and the only friend I had was a young woman with almost as few responsibilities. In a few short weeks I went from being an ascetic loner to being half of a hedonistic couple.

I tried everything but dancing. Alcohol, sex, drugs, violence. Rave parties, mosh pits. Every time I got into trouble, Hana was there to patch me up and misdirect the police. It was eventful, but none of the events yielded any sort of meaning. I craved sensation, stimulation–anything that would get me out of my own head. Anything that set lights pin-wheeling through my consciousness. Anything that diverted my attention from what I had lost.

While I did not make any friends, suddenly I was a member of a social circle. Everybody knew my name, and nobody hesitated to speak it. For my part, I rarely thought about killing any of them.

Hana did not expect me to work, but sometimes work came to me in the same way that it did to her. Some of those who called on Hana for favors were lowland practitioners. Chronomancers, geomancers, sorcerers, necromancers. Some of them were dabblers, some were gifted amateurs. One or two of them, I am sure, were as gifted as members of the Academy's faculty.

For these underground practitioners, information was a scarce and precious resource. Where true wisdom was written down, it was usually concealed in mystical nonsense. If anyone possessed a proper library of magical texts, I never heard of it. If anyone found a single grimoire filled with practical, workable knowledge, I never saw it.

In the lowlands, the Arts are passed down from master to student, through peer groups and cabals, through lodges and cults. The knowledge they shared was simply too valuable to record in some place it might be stolen.

And then there was me. From my years spent in the Biblioteca Tenebrae, I had plenty of unusual knowledge, and unusual people would pay unusual amounts of money for my expertise. I could not work their disciplines, but I had enough grounding from my time in the Library of Shadows to express concepts to them clearly and enough insight to suggest the questions they did not know to ask.

Some clients wanted to know where I had gleaned this knowledge. Some knew of the Library of Shadows and wanted to learn how I had found the place. Some of them knew the dangers and wanted to know how I had survived my visits there. On these topics I said nothing.

I tried to use these strange new arts for myself. I knew the theory. I had talent and discipline. What I did not have was the ability to channel power. If my name had never been taken in the first place, perhaps I could have learned to shape as these other adepts did, but the wounds from its restoration had scarred over and the power would not flow.

The summons arrived unaccompanied in the back of a taxi.

Usually, consulting jobs came as telephone calls to Hana, or by email, or by other means that she did not disclose. I had no phone, no email of my own. I did not care to be contacted. So it was doubly surprising when the taxi-born summons came addressed to me.

I was getting used to being named. In London, few people ever questioned my provenance. When people asked where I was from, I could say New York, and that was always sufficient. Still, it was a surprise to hear my name from someone I had not even met. I was developing a reputation.

I did not ask Hana to come with me, but there was no question that her presence was required. I was still not fit company for strangers.

The taxi took us to a narrow, five-story Victorian apartment building in Knightsbridge. The exterior of the building was Gothic Revival, but the interiors had been remodeled under the guidance of a Feng Shui master with an army of interior decorators at his beck and call.

The concierge ignored us as we crossed the lobby to the elevators. The doors opened immediately, and the button for the fourth floor was lit.

"Are you doing this?" I asked.

"No," said Hana.

The doors opened into an apartment. Ultramodern furniture in gray and black and beige. Hardwood floors. The adept who lived here owned the entire fourth floor as well as what had once been the fifth, which he'd had pulled down to double the ceiling height.

Our host was waiting near the entrance, although it took me a moment to spot him. His garments–slacks and a collared shirt–were the same pale gray as the walls, and it wasn't until he moved that I noticed him standing there. Beside me, Hana started. Rare was the glamour that could fool her eyes, but this was something more fundamental than mere illusion. Even with my own hobbled abilities I knew it.

"Mr. Quay. Ms. Hana. My name is Jacob." The adept had small, glinting, dark eyes. Though he was neither pale nor thin, there was something insubstantial about him. Something beyond diffident.

And he looked familiar. I was sure that I knew his name but had forgotten it. I had known his name, but not in the same way that I had known the names of my teachers and peers at the Academy. He was *familiar*, like someone I had once met.

"Nice to meet you, Jacob," said Hana. I did not greet him.

"Come inside," he said. "Would you like some tea? Perhaps something stronger?"

"No."

Hana looked at me, but with resignation rather than disapproval. "Yes, please," she said. "Tea would be lovely."

"This way, please."

In the parlor, Hana and I sat together on a sofa. I looked around while we waited for our host to prepare the tea. There were no decorations visible. No vases, no plants, no paperweights or souvenirs. A seven-foot-tall frame leaned against the fireplace. It was covered with a heavy blanket.

Hana leaned across and whispered, "I think he's *Jacob Verne.*"

I recognized the name, and I knew that it matched the face, but I did not know who Jacob Verne was.

"The actor," said Hana. "His new movie–his *face*– is plastered on every bus stop and Tube station in the city."

I remembered the movie poster now. Jacob Verne, multiple Academy Award winner. Greatest actor of his generation, or so the posters claimed. He was also, apparently, an adept of some standing.

"Oh," I replied. "That Jacob Verne."

Jacob returned with the teapot and two cups. I sat through the milk-and-sugar ritual impatiently. What was the purpose of it? We were here on business. I would make my own tea if I was thirsty.

Eventually, it was done. Hana sat back with her tea, and Jacob settled in the armchair with his own drink balanced on his knee.

"Mr. Quay," said Jacob, "I understand that you are a man of many talents."

I blinked slowly. "I have some expertise," I replied. "Talent is a different matter."

He nodded. "And power is different again."

I did not care to discuss how much power or talent I possessed, or once had. "What do you need from me?"

"I need you to save me," he said.

"What's wrong with you?"

"Look closely," he said. "You'll see."

My ability to perceive beyond my normal biological senses was mostly gone, so I turned to Hana. She looked at Jacob.

"You seem all right," she said, but hesitantly.

I looked at him again for a moment. "Show me your hands."

He held them out for inspection.

"You're right-handed," I said. I had seen him pour the tea. "But you wear your watch on your right wrist."

Hana looked sidelong at me. "Some people do."

"Not many." I leaned forward, took Jacob's wrist, and pulled the cuff back from the face of his watch. The twelve was at the top and the six at the bottom, but the three was on the left and the nine on the right. The watch face had been flopped from left to right.

"A mirror image," said Hana, looking at Jacob again. "Even your heart is on the right side."

"And yet he is still right-handed," I said. "Stand up."

He stood.

"Turn your back."

From behind he seemed less substantial than before. Not transparent, but less real.

"He's a reflection," said Hana.

Jacob nodded. "As you say. I am a mirror image."

"Mostly surface," I said.

"Yes," he replied. "The sliver of consciousness that inhabits...me...is itself only a shard."

"And the true Jacob?" said Hana.

I pointed a thumb at the covered frame. "He went through the mirror."

Jacob nodded. "We swapped places. Now I...he... is lost in the reflected world. I need you to bring me back."

"Why not go and find him yourself?"

Jacob pulled the blanket away to show us the mirror beneath. "I cannot," he said. "I have no reflection with which to trade places."

I stepped to the mirror and looked into it. It was rare for me to do so. I tried to look past my reflection, to see the image only as a pattern of reflected light. I was not the man in the glass–that was my father. Perhaps I would cut my hair, after all.

Hana moved to join me. I looked at her image, and then I looked at the surface of the mirror itself. "The frame is old," I said, "but the glass is new."

Hana looked at Jacob. "You replaced it after... he... went through. He broke it."

Jacob nodded slowly. "The spell was flawed. I could not reassemble the mirror from its shards."

"And the new glass won't show you at all," said Hana.

"Did you bleed?" I asked.

"In as much as this form is able, yes. It was only a small amount."

Hana put her hand on my arm.

"I see I have called upon the right people," said Jacob. The look on his face was plaintive. "Will you help me?"

"What's behind the glass?" I asked. "Can you describe the world that lies on the other side?"

He shook his head. "I don't know," he said. "I have no memory of it. A mirror is a two-dimensional plane. It's flat. There is nothing but reflected light. There is no consciousness, no life, no depth. It is not a place."

"But now there's a mind in there," I said. "Jacob Verne's mind."

"It is my own," said Jacob, "but I scarcely know it better than you do."

Hana and I looked at each other, and it was agreed.

We didn't ask Jacob for a price. It would be dangerous work and, if we succeeded, Jacob Verne would owe us forever. He would be beholden to us. His occult resources might be scant, but he was a man of wealth. In the temporal world, that is the strongest power there is.

———◖●◗———

Hana performed the rite. I didn't understand it—I couldn't see it properly with my sight blinkered. I think she found some echo...some reflection...of Jacob's original working and changed it. Adjusted some parameter, fixed some defect.

She turned to me when it was ready. "Can you still do this?"

Hana was the one who had taught me to project my consciousness beyond the range of my biological senses. I had learned the skill well enough, but that was in the time when I was unnamed, and my potential was without limit. Now I was defined entirely by my limitations.

"Yes, but it must be under your power," I said. "You will need to pull me with you. I can hold myself together well enough to navigate." I spoke with confidence, but I did not know if it was true. Would willpower suffice, or would my consciousness fray apart and blow away with no Art to hold it together? We would find out.

I felt no fear. I thought I had already suffered the worst thing that could be inflicted on me. If this was the end of me, who would care? Not I.

Hana took my hand, and together we stepped into the glass.

Stepping through the mirror was diminishing. As I rotated through the transformation, I felt as though I was being hollowed out. There was no chill, but the temperature fell away. The concepts of warmth and cold became irrelevant.

Once through the barrier, Hana and I stood facing the direction we had come from: back out of the mirror. The real world was a bright rectangle in the gray dimness. The pane of glass we had come through was unbroken. That was good. We would probably not suffer Jacob's fate. I wondered what other dangers might await us.

I turned away from the glass, but Hana lingered. "Come on," I said. I was still holding her hand, and I pulled on it. She looked at me, disturbed, and then followed.

We were in a version of Jacob's living room. Perspective broke as I turned my head about. The angles were wrong. Straight lines oscillated like waveforms. Any motion of my head tore and blurred the landscape, slashing it open with specular knives. The torn edges closed up if I kept still, but the parallax distortions remained.

I was insubstantial, though I was more solid than the world I now inhabited. I felt a measure of the diffidence that Jacob had shown. My motivation, my confidence. The core of me was eroding.

"Where is he?" said Hana. "Can you find him?"

"This world is no bigger than the mirror surface–finding him is not the problem. Making him communicate will be more difficult."

I moved around the couch, past the mantelpiece and toward the doorway. Hana came too. If I let go of her hand, I would be shunted out of the mirror world, back into the meat of me...probably. Perhaps my self would just simply vanish, and my life would be over. I did not find either prospect to be particularly distressing.

Through the doorway, the world was dimmer yet. The vestibule and its contents were well represented, but as I moved out of the half-space, the representation blurred to gray mist. Fractured, phantasmal objects were visible in the dimness, flickering in and out of existence: a lamp, a potted plant, a traffic light. Random objects, many times reflected, that happened to glance off some corner of the big mirror in Jacob's parlor.

"Here," I said.

"Quay, we have to stay in sight of the exit," said Hana, holding tight to my hand.

"Jacob has gone to a place beyond the reflection," I replied. "You stay in sight of the glass. I'll go and find him." I took a hard left out of the half-space and into the gray mist. Within two steps it had darkened to black.

I was still holding onto Hana's hand, but I could no longer see it. My right arm, as best I could perceive, ended somewhere below the elbow.

I had gone beyond the bend of the light, but I was unconcerned. If there is one thing I am good at, it is finding my way in the dark.

In the Library of Shadows there was no light, but there was knowledge available for those who had the capacity to receive it. That, in its way, was a kind of illumination. This place inside the mirror, beyond its arc of view, contained no information. It was the emptiest place I had ever ventured.

That was where Jacob Verne was hiding. Squatting naked in the darkness, hugging his knees, his face turned away.

"Jacob," I said. "You sent for help. We have come."

Jacob did not look at me. "That wasn't me," he said. His voice was tremulous and thin. "That was something who only thinks it is."

"It knows what it is. It is you, though perhaps only a single aspect. It wants me to help you."

He did not turn his head. "I am beyond help. Beyond salvation."

"I can take you back through the glass."

"Perhaps you can," said Jacob, "but that would not save me."

"Why is that?"

"I...am empty." He turned to me then, and I saw it on his face. "I am not a person. I am just a succession of faces, cast upon a mirror of skin."

Faults darkened and spread across Verne's face. As I watched, the lines became cracks, the cracks became fissures. There was a tinkling, grinding noise as he forced the shards back together, trying to keep his identity from splintering apart. Nevertheless, pieces splintered off. Gaps were visible—and growing.

He looked away again. "Do you know who I am?"

"You're Jacob Verne, the movie star."

I didn't know if I had seen any of his movies, but I had the idea that Verne was the kind of actor who disappeared into the role. You might see ten of his movies and never recognize him for the same man, unless you knew to look.

"I'm Jacob Verne," he said. He pronounced his name carefully, as he might words from a foreign tongue. "The actor."

I waited for him to continue.

"I chose this," he said. "I suppose it was a foregone conclusion. All those characters, all those roles..."

"You became so many people that you could no longer find Jacob inside yourself."

"I was never sure if I was me, or just some character I was playing."

"You thought you could find yourself in the mirror."

"I hoped to." Again he looked at me, and now his face was different. It was still Jacob's face, but the man inhabiting it was someone else. A fool. Wide eyes, a question mark of a mouth. "But I was too fragile, and my questioning smashed me all to pieces." His voice had changed subtly, some shift in timbre and accent. Hana would have appreciated the difference better than I did.

"You put yourself back together," I said.

Jacob turned away. I heard the crunching glass as he came apart and reformed. The master thespian had no way to communicate if he was not performing. When he turned back, he had become someone else again. A wise man. A wizard. Hooded eyes, quivering lips. "I put the pieces back together, but there are gaps. The bonds are broken. The *I* cannot be repaired. The...me...inside..." He spoke with knowledge, but his voice quavered with infirmity.

Slivers of glass fell out his head as he turned it away. "I saw what was inside," he said. Now his voice was brittle. "What was at the core." He swallowed, a painful, glassy sound. "There was only darkness. There was only nothing."

"That is because a mirror can only reflect the surface." I held out my empty left hand. "Come with us, and we will restore you to flesh and blood. You will know you have depth when you can once again bleed."

But Jacob wasn't listening anymore, if ever he had been. More shards fell from the shell of him.

I could feel my own identity starting to crack. I stepped back and away, clasping my left hand to my right. Hana caught the signal and pulled me toward her. The darkness thinned to murk, and there was Hana, staring concernedly.

"Quickly." I pulled her arm and lunged toward the mirror. Two steps, three, then five. I could hear the tinkling of breaking glass all around us. The brightness of the mirror-face reared before us, and we went through.

Jacob's reflection was gone when we stepped back through into the parlor. The tea he had served sat cooling on the silver tray, but there was otherwise nothing to show that he had ever been in the room.

I glanced back at the mirror, and my hated reflection glanced back at me. Hana kept her back to the glass. She was shivering.

"He's gone," I said. "There's nothing left."

"Even the...the meat?"

I nodded. "The image was reflected too many times," I said. "Too much data lost."

Hana shuddered. "What happened in there?"

I told her what I had seen, what he had said.

"He looked inside himself and found nothing there," she said. "Poor man."

I shook my head. "No," I said. "He found something; he just couldn't accept it."

"What did he find, Quay? What did he see that was so horrible it made him wither up and die?"

"Same thing that's inside everyone." I let go of Hana's hand. "Blood and shadow."

Act 12.

— BLOOD AND SHADOW —

Hana and I returned to the share-house to find our room full of spider webs.

The week since our journey through Jacob Verne's mirror had passed in a narcotic haze. This time, though, it was Hana who wanted to consume. To forget. I did not know what she had seen in that mirror, but something had spooked her. Whatever had provoked the binge, I was happy to participate.

I was drunk and tripping when we returned to Hana's place after a night on the town that could easily have ended up a night in police custody. As I blundered into the darkness, there was a sensation of those silken filaments on my skin. At first, I thought it was a hallucination, but three steps in, I found myself ensnared. By the time I thought to cry out, Hana, too, was caught in the web.

I'd been in London for more than a year. I had come to think of that room as a place of safety, although I did not think Hana had set any wards upon it. Wards were a concern of my past life. Since my return I had few considerations but for the present moment.

But it wouldn't have mattered if the room had been properly secured. I remembered how easily Arakne had slipped through my best defenses back at the Academy, and I wondered how powerful she had become in the intervening years.

"Hello, Quay. Hana."

I flinched to hear her speak my name, though it did me no harm. I could not locate her in the darkness.

I tried to reply, but a skein of web sealed my mouth shut. I issued a muffled grunt and fell silent.

"This is how you greet old friends?" said Hana.

"You were once my friend," said Arakne. Her voice was coming from above us. "But *this* one? He's never had a friend in his life and never will."

"He's all right now."

There was something massive hanging from the ceiling. I could make out a bulbous shape, gleaming mirror-eyes, and long, many-jointed arms. The shape lowered itself toward me for a closer look. The web filaments that secured me tightened, rotating me toward it for inspection.

I stared with dilated eyes. I stank of alcohol and sweat. I felt like the burned end of a discarded match.

"I think 'pathetic' is closer to the mark," said the spider.

Hana paused. "Well, a bit of that, yeah. But he's harmless now."

"Indeed." Mandibles clacked inches from my face. I could not move.

The light switch flipped on and the web that held me immobile fell away. I stumbled, caught myself. Shaded my eyes against the brightness.

Arakne was sitting cross-legged on the mattress. She looked her old self but grown up. The reflector eyes were gone, and so were the mandibles and the spinnerets and the retinue of tiny spiders that used to float about her on loose strands of web. Even the spider tattoo on her neck was covered by her collar. Having abandoned her affectations, Arakne looked more dangerous than ever.

"I should kill you," she said. "Both of you. Kill you and eat you, just to be safe."

"Is that why you came here?" asked Hana.

"Yes." Arakne hesitated. "Well, yes and no. Eating you wasn't a part of the original plan, but you've been out for a long time, and I am getting hungry."

She turned to me. "Have you anything to say?"

The web over my mouth fell away. "I could say your name," I slurred.

"It would do you no good," said Arakne. "And then I would definitely have to kill both of you."

Hana looked at me. "You know her name?"

"Yes."

"How?"

Arakne spoke for me. "His father, of course. Professor Quay implanted every name he knew in the boy. Just in case."

"In case of what?" said Hana.

Arakne rolled her eyes. I hadn't seen her do that since I had first met her. Her real eyes were so much darker than I remembered. "In case he needed them."

"My father is dead," I said, "and I'm tired of hearing about him. Why are you here?" I hoped it was for sex. Some part of me that was not intoxicated knew that it was not–but I hoped there would be sex, anyway.

"The Chancellor came to me," she said. "He invited me back to the Academy."

"And you refused," said Hana. She sat down on the mattress across from Arakne.

"He told me that he had restored the place to order. With this Quay exiled and Thieu gone, the Faction had fallen apart. He guaranteed there would be no reprisals from those I betrayed."

I couldn't come up with anything coherent to say. I supposed that Hana could have restored me to sobriety, if she had wanted to. I was glad she had not.

"So why did you refuse?" asked Hana.

Arakne looked away. "Because I don't trust him, and because I'm starting to think I chose the wrong side. The Academy still squats on its mountaintop, holding itself above the rest of us. Keeping its lineage *pure*." She spat the word. "Keeping us lowlanders under its yoke."

I wonder if the Chancellor knew that Arakne and Hana had rescued me from the mountaintop. I wondered if he cared.

Hana stared at her. "But...Professor Quay wanted to..."

"Professor Quay wanted to open the doors, to turn over the system. He wanted to change it," said Arakne.

"He wanted to rule over every lowland practitioner, as well as all those at the Academy. He wanted to be the Archimage."

Arakne shrugged. "Well, of course he did. That was why I opposed him. But we could, perhaps, have dealt with Professor Quay in the chaos. Now, with the Chancellor still in his chair and no opposition left to challenge him, there is no hope for a change."

Hana turned to me. "I don't suppose you know the Chancellor's name?"

The question surprised me. My mind was still in a narcotic blur, and I had difficulty introspecting the answer. "No," I said.

"Of course he doesn't," said Arakne. "If his father had managed to learn it, we would never have been in this situation."

"But...how did he learn all the names in the first place?" said Hana.

"What do you think Professor Quay was doing when he took those furloughs from the Academy? He was studying everyone. Tracing us back to our former lives. Turning over every clue he had about our origins and cross-referencing it to children reported missing, all over the world."

"I thought those furloughs were about...him." Hana nodded her head toward me.

Arakne nodded. "Yes, they were about him, too. That was Professor Quay's other major project."

"My father is *dead*," I said. It was all I could think of. "I am my own person now, with my own needs."

Arakne snorted and waved a hand dismissively. "You are nothing," she said. "You don't even have your own name. If Hana here had not made a toy of you, you would have died on the slopes and been forgotten. Your precious *needs* are a distant echo of your father's, and you yourself are less even than that."

Now I was angry. "I am nobody's toy!" I turned to Hana, but she would not look at me.

"Oh yes, you are. You're a tame version of someone she feared. Someone over whom she exercises power. You are Quay, are you not?"

There were tears in Hana's eyes when she looked at me. "It's not true, Quay," she said. "Maybe it was, at first. Maybe just a little. But I..."

"You pitied him," said Arakne.

"*You* brought him to me. I took him in my arms when the rest of you feared him."

"You should fear me still," I mumbled, but Arakne spoke over me.

"We did fear him, Hana. Of course we did. All of us. The dark prince who destroyed his own father. The psycho who disappeared into the Library of Shadows for years at a time. Nobody knew what he had inherited. What he'd learned. What he was capable of. And he *looked* just like the old man." Thieu had never spoken to me with such contempt as I heard in Arakne's voice. "But in the end, he had nothing. Just a handful of names and that sulky black stare of his."

"I had power," I insisted. "I destroyed Saad. I defeated Professor Thieu."

"You had power," said Arakne, "but not like your father. You had a vicious cunning and a handful of tricks and, somehow, you used them to defeat men who were stronger, smarter, and wiser than you. But now? Now you are just a broken thing. You will never be the man your father was."

"I never wanted to be."

"That choice was never yours to make."

My mind was beginning to clear. I could see the curvature of what she was saying, but it was too big and too close for me to discern the true shape of it. "What do you mean?"

Hana covered her face with her hands. "You really don't know?"

"Tell me."

Arakne pressed her hands together and pointed them at me. "You are your father. Do you understand me?" She said it in the same tone of voice that the Chancellor had used when he had asked me that question. "You and he are the same person, on a genetic level. You have the same DNA. I do not know if your mother was ever a part of you, or if he fashioned your embryo entirely from himself, but by the time you were born he had flushed her genome from you entirely. You are him, and him only. You are a clone. A copy. A doppelganger."

I leaned back against the wall. Suddenly, I wished I had Arakne's web to hold me up against the swell of nausea. The alcohol in my stomach churned. I felt as if my eyes were spinning independently of each other.

"I was to be his backup."

"Precisely. That's why he kept you isolated and alone. That's why he protected you. If something happened to him, he was going to decant his consciousness into your body, and that would have been the end of Quay Junior."

I remembered my final confrontation with my father; how he had asked me to open my defenses to him so that he could be restored. He had practically told me his intentions.

"You weren't meant to be a person," said Arakne. "You were never more than a spare suit of clothes."

"The names were an insurance policy, to keep me alive in case something went wrong and he was prevented from taking possession immediately."

"Yes. It was a good plan. I think it would have worked, too, if you hadn't followed him that time. When the Chancellor saw you together, he knew what your father planned. So did the Faction."

I sank to the floor with my back against the wall as the knowledge permeated my drug-addled brain.

I never had a chance at the Academy. The Faction could never trust me because the Chancellor had saved me and brought me into the school. Those who sided with the Chancellor could never trust me because I was literally a re-embodiment of their enemy.

The Chancellor had known all of this. He had used me to destroy the Faction, and then he had cast me aside.

"How did you find us?" asked Hana. "I told you we would be in New York."

"You were the last people to see Jacob Verne alive, and you didn't think anyone would hear about it?"

"No," said Hana. "I thought I had covered our tracks well enough."

Arakne's laugh was accompanied by a clacking sound. "I am the spider, my graceful little nose-flower," she said. "Though you cannot see my web, it is wide, and its harvest is bountiful."

Hana stood up. "Spiders are useful for controlling pests," she said. "But nobody wants one in their home. Many of them are poisonous, and all of them are ugly."

Even though I was still half-drunk, I could feel the power gathering between Arakne and Hana.

"Hey," I said. I drew myself unsteadily upright. "Hey."

When Arakne and Hana turned their attention to me, I grinned sloppily and licked my lips. "Are we going to have a threesome now?"

Arakne's eyes narrowed. "I wondered what it would be like if you ever smiled, Quay," she said. "Now I'm sorry I found out."

She pushed me aside and went through the door. I fell in a heap. "Enjoy your wretched lives, arseholes. I doubt they will last much longer."

When I had recovered myself enough to get up, the spider was long gone.

I turned back to Hana. She put her hands over her mouth, then her eyes. "Oh, Quay," she said. "Quay. I'm so sorry."

She reached for me, but I turned my back on her.

"Quay..."

"Hana," I said. "When we stepped through Jacob Verne's mirror, and you looked back into the glass, what did you see?"

She hesitated. "I saw my reflection," she said.

"Was it your reflection, or was it the real you, standing on the other side of the glass?"

"The real me."

"What else did you see?"

"You were right there beside me. You saw what I did."

"I was *right there beside you*. What did you see, Hana?"

She said nothing. I turned to face her once more.

"What did you see?"

"I saw you, Quay," she said. "I saw you there, standing beside me."

"Did you see my reflection," I asked, "Or did you see my father's?"

This time Hana turned her face away. I knew what she would say before she spoke.

"All I saw was your shadow."

Act 13.

— SHADOWMANCY —

I needed to get out of London. I did not know who else might come looking for me, but it was clear that I was known, and I still had plenty of enemies–both my own, and my father's. I had little choice but to flee.

I had left Brooklyn as a minor: I had no documents, no money, no contacts. There was no way for me to prove my civilian identity. That was good. I was underground, and I needed to stay that way. But it made it difficult to travel.

My only remaining resource was the scrap of power I had hoarded away since my banishment. But I had been named: I could no longer channel that power properly. Once I removed the dressing, it would drain freely and I would never be able to draw more.

I didn't think it would all gush away at once. I would probably be able to utilize some of it as it bled out, like a car with a hole in the fuel tank. I was less certain that there was enough fuel for me to get to my destination, but I resolved to try. I had little enough choice.

I was going home.

I walked from Hana's squat with no regard for direction. I just needed to get away. I did not know who might be surveilling our place, and I wanted to get clear of them before I began my working.

I went two kilometers...three...before I felt that I had gone far enough to elude most casual observers. If anyone had set a more formal enchantment, they would probably have cast it all across the city.

I came to the river. I walked along the banks of the Thames toward Greenland Pier. The terminal was closed up now; it was still hours before the first of the morning clippers was due. Lights smudged the surface of the river, but the water continued heedless, a slow dark serpent crawling to the abyss of the sea.

This was far enough.

I shut my eyes and straightened my arms at my sides, raised my hands a few inches from my thighs with fingers splayed. I exhaled the shadowstuff I had used to staunch the wound the Chancellor had inflicted upon me fourteen months earlier.

Once again, the power flowed through me. It was thrilling and shocking. The raw pulse of it burned at the fringes of my psyche. The resistance my named identity provided gave rise to increased voltage. Too much of it would quickly overload me; burn out my mind like the filament in a light bulb.

I threw my working into the current and hoped it would hold together in the chop.

It bore me up. London dwindled beneath me as I passed into the clouds, and then through them. In the far distance, to the east, a range of mountains stood between me and the rising sun. Its radiance spread toward me, lighting the sea of clouds in golds and reds. My enemies were there in those mountains. The Academy. The Chancellor.

I turned my back on them and stepped out onto the red-gold vapor. I started walking, but I could not outpace the dawn. The golden rays caught up to me, and my Art began to falter. Then I was falling.

Down, through the darkening gray clouds. Lightning coruscated through rippling storm front. Rain lashed my skin. Hail beat against my bones. My shadow streamed about me, tattered and billowing.

I lit on the ocean in a cone of vapor. Shadows hardened beneath my feet, and I strode through the salt spray. In the distance I could see the radiance of the city. My city.

Night fell, and suddenly I was a child again. My father loomed in the black and starless sky, huge and forbidding, robes flapping about him. His eyes were black and empty. In his hands he held the Chancellor's book.

He promised me everything, once again. He promised the Chancellorship he had coveted. He promised me every secret, every power, every Mystery. He swore his promise on the Chancellor's book of names, on his love for me as his son and heir.

But the book of names was a fake, and my father was dead, and I...

I was a grown man, and I was dangerous yet.

It was past midnight by the time I arrived in New York.

Battery Park. I had been here only once, in the company of my father. We had walked along the Esplanade and all the way from the North Cove marina to the rough walls of Castle Clinton. It had been autumn, then, and the sky was cold and bright. The trees were red and orange. Now it was summer, and the grass was lush. The foliage was dark against the hot neon sky.

I stepped out of the water and onto the guardrail and stared up at the city. The Empire State Building. The strange black monolith that had replaced the twin towers of the old World Trade Center. The Statue of Liberty stood behind me, up-lit by dozens of floodlights. Dramatic shadows hung over her face and shoulders, like a shawl.

I had only a tiny amount of power remaining to me. I folded it up with a snatch of shadow and stuffed it into my heart.

I changed the pounds sterling in my pocket to dollars at a 24-hour money exchanger. There wasn't much: I spent most of it on a hamburger and a bottle of water. I did not care how it tasted. All I wanted was something to silence the hunger pangs.

From the diner, I descended into the subway. I was shocked by the familiar smell of it. Metal fatigue and urine and static electricity.

Not much had changed down in the subway. The turnstiles would no longer accept tokens, but they were just as easy to evade as I remembered. By the time I arrived in Brooklyn, the nostalgia had worn off. I was home.

I got off at my stop and took the eastern exit, as I always had with my father. I went up the stairs and turned right, toward my street.

My block was gone. The school, the market, the delicatessen–all of it. In its place was a solid wall of new glass and fresh concrete, flushed and squared, with only panels of pre-molded fascia to differentiate the individual buildings. Apartment blocks, shop fronts, cafes. A Comfort Inn stood on the lot my parents' house had once occupied, and a convenience store named 24-Seven stood roughly where the market once had been, complete with an orange-green-red logo made to trick the unwary into thinking it was a genuine 7-Eleven. I went inside.

The 24-Seven clerk sang the name of each of my purchases as he rang them up. "Two fifths of Wild Turkey...four cans of Boston beans...half a dozen razorblades." He smiled at me and said, "Having a bit of a party, are we, sir?"

"Yes."

The clerk had no more questions. When the amount came up on the register, he did not read it aloud. It came to sixteen dollars eighty, but I shorted him the ten. Six dollars eighty was all the currency I possessed. Again.

I could smell a storm coming.

I took a room at the Comfort Inn. I didn't check in; I just took it. I walked right past the reception, rode the elevator to the top floor, and let myself into an unoccupied suite.

Outside, the storm built to a fury. I suppose it was a hurricane. I did not notice the lights outside my window go out, but at some point the storm caused a city-wide blackout. The elevator stopped working, as well as the ice machine, the air conditioner, the television and the alarm clock. I don't know if the hotel staff even knew that I was in that room, but nobody came to my door to advise me that the city was being evacuated.

I would not have left. If I had, the storm would have gone with me.

It took me four days to design and script the working. Four days sitting in the darkness, with only the forking lightning to illuminate my room.

I ate the beans when my body needed sustenance. I drank the bourbon when I felt doubts about what I was planning. I worked steadily and without sleep until the spell was ready.

I sat on the edge of the bed, my shirt off and my shoes long discarded. I drank the last of the bourbon in three long swallows.

These were the last dregs of my power. If this working failed, I would be truly destitute.

I set the empty bottle down carefully on the windowsill, lined up with its twin and the four empty cans. I drew my legs under me and raised my head.

I had barely enough magic left to work the razors. They rose from the open box and circled me like wary hornets.

The Academy teaches us to work in silence. Only proper names may be spoken; all other elements of a working must be contained in the mind of the practitioner. But the working I designed in the darkened city owed little to the Arts I had learned in the Academy's halls.

I opened my mouth and spoke the words I needed to say: "My skin is a door, to be unlocked and opened."

I lowered my head as the razors did their work, carving their patterns into my flesh. I clawed my fingers against the pain. The cutting continued.

"My heart is the room of the past. My shadow is the room of the future. My blood is the path that shows me the way."

I could feel the shadows writhing beneath my skin, coiling and twisting, branching and thickening like the roots of a weed.

"I open the door. I welcome the darkness. I tread its path."

Black tendrils curled from my eyes, my nose, my ears, from the network of lines and symbols cut into my flesh. They drew me up off the mattress until I hung suspended in the air, flopping like a fish on a gaff.

"For I am blood and skin, but I would be shadow."

———— ❰ ● ❱ ————

The Chancellor was right, of course.

The shadow of my lineage was long upon me. By drawing it into my being–by naming it as I myself am named–I made it greater yet.

In the Arts of the Academy, the magician stands outside of the natural order of things. He separates the internal world from the external. If he can name a thing, he can induce changes upon it. He himself must be unnamed in order to occupy the position from which he can act. These arts are lost to me now–but they are not the only powers in the world.

Most of the shadow-play I had demonstrated at the Academy was just that–play. I had used my shadow to give the ideas shape because it felt comfortable after all the time I had spent in the Biblioteca Tenebrae, but those workings had been rendered with the Academy's own principles: the Naming Art. They were not true shadowmancy.

Shadowmancy is an inversion of the Naming Art. The shadowmancer is cast upon the world, and he must act upon the environment from his own point of view. The shadowmancer's internal world is not discrete: it bleeds out into the external world; it extends beyond the boundaries of the shadowmancer's embodied will.

The Naming Art of the Academy is unnamed, as its practitioners must be. They are direct and coercive. They resist description in any terms but their own. They are the arts of truth. Truth is irrefutable, regardless of the logical calculus with which it is reasoned.

The art of shadowmancy is instead concerned with metaphor. It is a way of asserting power over a situation by imposing a new frame of reference upon it, by matching reality and then altering it by distortions of perspective. For who can know truth? Who can truly perceive reality, with such a flawed and imprecise instrument as the human mind?

Shadowmancy is the art obscuring the truth in order to persuade reality to match your lies.

A shadow is a real thing, though it has no mass or volume. With the right instruments, and the right mathematics, you can deduce much about the world by examining the fall of its shadows.

A shadow may not stand free of its context, but it can assume any shape, any size; it can merge with any other shadow and then return to its own fluid boundaries.

In order to change the shadow of a thing you must change the parameters by which it is cast: the direction of the light; the size and orientation and motion of the objects that occlude it.

The art of shadowmancy makes this principle commutative. If you change the shadow of something, you must change the context in which it is cast by adding your shadow to its own.

The shadowmancer puts the darkness first. The shadowmancer must, himself, become a shadow.

Thus transformed, I left my room. I blew down through the streets and out toward Coney Island. A strange gust of wind in the still night air drew me down over the boardwalk until I stood at the very end of it, looking out across the sea. The storm had passed, and only the barest points of brightness shone down from the empty sky.

On a clear day I would have been able to see Sandy Hook Point across the water, but not at night. And certainly not this night.

The sea before me was not the Coney Island Channel. I stood facing some other kind of ocean, blacker than the void of space, and deeper. An ocean filled not with water, but with raw and formless darkness.

No ship can sail upon that sea. No submarine can plumb its depths. It is broad without limit, deep beyond measure. Nothing may cross that sea, but, if one has the art, anything may be drawn from it.

I drew the place I wished to me.

It was as easy as fishing from a quay.

And here I stand, on the plateau beneath the Academy.

The white marble ziggurat shines bright above me, though the sky is black, and there are no stars in it. My shadow spills up the steps, massive and misshapen.

The Chancellor waits above me. He has the entire school assembled behind him: every professor, every sensei, every doctor and master and savant and acolyte. Maruyama and Boudreaux and all the others; the old guard whose names I know, and the new cohort, whose names I do not. They stand in a phalanx: ranks and files aligned into a wedge, with the Chancellor at its point.

I mount the stairs, a black and hulking thing. Shadows ooze from where they have burst open my flesh. Splintered ribs protrude from the dark mass of my torso. Loops of intestines dangle free where they spill from my ruptured belly.

My shadow flexes, and the remains of my skin ruck up across my shoulders, ragged and split. I have no face. I have no shape. I am an unbordered blot of darkness, bleeding into my own projected shadow.

I will never possess the Mysteries. I no longer want them. I do not want what the Academy has to offer. I do not want revenge. I do not want dominion over nature or supremacy over my enemies.

I just want to hear them speak my name.

— ACKNOWLEDGEMENTS —

Shadowmancy began its unnatural life as a comic, and it started at the end.

Nic Hunter is to blame, of course. He challenged me to write that original script quickly, so that he could be in the first issue of my Kagemono horror anthology series, which at the time was just about ready to print. I didn't think there was any way he could manage it. Not only did he smash the deadline, but his lush artwork has informed the characters and the direction of the story in countless ways. So first and foremost, my thanks go out to Nic. It was a pleasure to work with you.

That original short was published in 2008 in Kagemono #1. It's a 6-page story that begins at the point where Quay is expelled from the Academy and ends where this novel does. Obviously I have expanded it since then. But I knew that there was more of the story to tell, and with such a powerful artist bringing it to life I was very keen to write more. So we went back to what is now the start of the book, "The Key in the Wall." This opening chapter was published in the final Kagemono volume in 2010, and then reprinted in Terra Magazine #1 in 2012.

At that point my intention was to tell the story in six installments, but Terra Magazine folded after that first issue and the second completed chapter was never published. It was another year before I decided to turn the comic into a short story, which grew into a novella, which grew into the book you have just finished (unless you skipped straight to the Acknowledgements, but what kind of a magical sociopath would do that?).

That's a long and complicated journey for such a short book, and there are many other people who have helped me navigate the twists and turns along the way.

Big thanks to Marta Salek, for beta-reading and for endless encouragement. This was a difficult book to write and an even more difficult one to like, and Marta countered all of my emailed whining with undeserved sympathy and unfailing support.

Cheers also to Stephen Ormsby, for acquiring this when it was a half-written disaster, and then convincing me not only to finish it, but to expand it to its full potential.

Muchas gracias to my compadre Jason Fischer for the unlimited supply of puns and laughter while I was putting the finishing touches on this rather grim undertaking.

Thanks to Jeremy Mohler from Outland Entertainment for taking a chance on the book, and to Scott Colby for his razor sharp edits for this second edition.

Finally, I must acknowledge the late, great Ursula K. Le Guin. Ursula's work has been an immeasurable influence over me since I was 9 years old, and I think my debt to her is particularly obvious here in Shadowmancy. There was never a better writer in any genre and, if you haven't read her work yet, I encourage you to rectify that immediately.

Start anywhere, except the end.

— Jason Franks, Melbourne, 2022